Ian Maclaren, William Winter, Henry Irving

**A Wreath of Laurel**

being speeches on dramatic and kindred occasions

Ian Maclaren, William Winter, Henry Irving

**A Wreath of Laurel**
*being speeches on dramatic and kindred occasions*

ISBN/EAN: 9783337340131

Printed in Europe, USA, Canada, Australia, Japan

Cover: Foto ©Andreas Hilbeck / pixelio.de

More available books at **www.hansebooks.com**

# A Wreath of Laurel

## BEING SPEECHES ON DRAMATIC AND KINDRED OCCASIONS

BY

WILLIAM WINTER

Publications of The Dunlap Society. New Series No. 7.
New York, 1898.

This is one of an edition of two hundred and sixty-five copies printed from type for the Dunlap Society in the month of November, 1898.

*Theo. L. DeVinne & Co.*

F. HERSTADT, ARTOTYPE.                    FROM A PASTEL BY J. WELLS CHAMPNEY. 1898.

Ever Faithfully Yours
William Winter

# A WREATH OF LAUREL

BEING

SPEECHES ON DRAMATIC
AND KINDRED OCCASIONS

BY

WILLIAM WINTER

NEW YORK
THE DUNLAP SOCIETY
1898

TO

# EDMUND CLARENCE STEDMAN

WHOSE FINE GENIUS AND EXQUISITE ART
HAVE ILLUMINED AND ADORNED
MORE THAN FORTY YEARS OF AMERICAN LITERATURE

I DEDICATE THIS BOOK

WITH HONOR FOR HIS ACHIEVEMENT
WITH GRATITUDE FOR HIS EXAMPLE
AND WITH AFFECTIONATE REMEMBRANCE
OF HIS LIFELONG FRIENDSHIP

## WILLIAM WINTER

*July 15, 1898*

# CONTENTS

## I

## Dramatic Speeches

PAGE

I. HENRY IRVING AND THE DRAMA.
SPEECH AND POEM AT A PEN AND PENCIL
CLUB FESTIVAL IN HONOR OF HENRY
IRVING, AT THE WATERLOO HOTEL,
EDINBURGH, OCTOBER 31, 1894 . . 1

II. IAN MACLAREN: POETRY AND PATHOS IN
SCOTTISH LITERATURE.
SPEECH AND POEM AT A FESTIVAL IN
HONOR OF IAN MACLAREN (DR. JOHN
WATSON) GIVEN BY THE LOTOS CLUB,
NEW YORK, DECEMBER 6, 1896 . . . 15

III. THE STAGE AND ITS APOSTLES.
SPEECH AND POEM DELIVERED BEFORE
THE LOTOS CLUB, NEW YORK, AT A
FESTIVAL GIVEN BY THE CLUB, IN HONOR
OF THE SPEAKER, APRIL 24, 1897 . . 27

IV. THE INTELLECTUAL STANDARD IN ACTING
AND WRITING.
SPEECH DELIVERED BEFORE THE ACTORS'
FUND SOCIETY, AT THE GARRICK THEA-
TRE, NEW YORK, JUNE 8, 1897 . . . 41

# Contents.

PAGE

V. The Ancient Glories of the Roman Catholic Church.
Speech and Poem at a Festival in Honor of Judge Joseph F. Daly, given by the Catholic Club, New York, November 6, 1897 . . . . . 51

VI. Joseph Jefferson: The Poet and the Actor.
Speech and Poem at a Festival in Honor of Joseph Jefferson, given by the Colonial Club, New York, March 31, 1898 . . . . . . . . 59

II

## Academic Speeches

I. Youth and Opportunity.
Speech delivered at the Theatre in Stapleton, Staten Island, June 19, 1891 . . . . . . . . . . . 73

II. The Ideal in Education.
Speech delivered at the Theatre in Stapleton, Staten Island, June 17, 1892 . . . . . . . . . . . 87

# Contents.

PAGE

III. THE TRUTH IN EULOGY.
SPEECH DELIVERED ON CURTIS MEMO-
RIAL DAY, AT THE STATEN ISLAND
ACADEMY, FEBRUARY 25, 1895  .  .  .  99

IV. THE IDEAL IN LIFE.
SPEECH DELIVERED AT THE THEATRE
IN STAPLETON, STATEN ISLAND, JUNE
18, 1895  .  .  .  .  .  .  .  .  .  .  .  107

V. IN MEMORY OF GEORGE WILLIAM CURTIS.
SPEECH DELIVERED AT THE SEMINARY
BUILDING, NEW BRIGHTON, STATEN IS-
LAND, FEBRUARY 24, 1896  .  .  .  .  .  117

VI. THE STATEN ISLAND ACADEMY.
A WORD OF WELCOME.—THE INTEL-
LECTUAL PRINCIPLE.— A WORD OF
FAREWELL.—SPEECHES DELIVERED AT
THE STATEN ISLAND ACADEMY, JUNE 15
AND JUNE 16, 1896.  .  .  .  .  .  .  .  129

RECORD OF NAMES  .  .  .  .  .  .  .  .  143

# PREFACE.

ASSOCIATES of mine in the Dunlap Society, being desirous of another book from my pen, have approved this collection of my comparatively recent speeches, and I now offer it with the hope that members of the Society in general, and other readers to whom it may come, will accept it, if not with entire approbation, at least with kindly tolerance.

Some of these speeches relate to dramatic subjects, and others, not specifically dramatic, which I have ventured to include, relate to kindred subjects, because they descant on the study of human experience and the conduct of human life. The Academic Speeches, constituting Part Second of the volume, are included for the reason that, as souvenirs of a writer long and intimately associated with the stage, they may commend themselves to the favor of theatrical readers; and also for the reason that they relate to a Library, founded by me, which is opulent with dramatic and musical books, and other artistic treasures, and which, by particular ordainment, is accessible to members of the dramatic profession.

Reference may appropriately be made, in this place, to earlier volumes of my speeches, to which this is a companion. My oration on " The Press and the Stage," delivered before the Goethe Society, at the

Brunswick Hotel, New York, January 28, 1889, was originally published in "Harper's Weekly," March 23, 1889, and afterward was put into a book: only 250 copies of it were made, and that book is out of print. My oration on "The Actor, and his Duty to his Time," was delivered before the Actors' Fund Society, at Palmer's Theatre, New York, June 4, 1889, and it was published in "Harper's Weekly" the next day. Messrs. Harper & Brothers, at all times considerate of authors, generously waived their claim of copyright, and sanctioned a reprint of both those works. The later and a few companions constitute Number Thirteen of the first series of the publications of the Dunlap Society, having been issued, under the title of "The Actor, and Other Speeches," in 1891. On February 24, 1893, at the Castleton, St. George, Staten Island, I delivered an oration commemorative of George William Curtis, and that was published, a little later, by Messrs. Macmillan & Co. The present, accordingly, is the fourth volume of my speeches.

I have never pretended to be an orator, I never liked to meet or to see crowds of people, and I never was conscious of a desire to convert anybody to my way of thinking, on any subject whatever. Orators aim to convince and to sway; my aim has been to extol genius, to celebrate nobility, to declare the worship of beauty, and, if possible, to diffuse a soothing and elevating charm of poetic grace. In my youth, in 1856, impelled by the political enthusiasm of that storm-swept time, I became a speaker for Fremont, in the presidential campaign against Buchanan, and sub-

sequently I delivered lectures at New England ly-
ceums, and so the art of public speaking became more
or less a custom.

The favor accorded to these speeches when they
were spoken encourages me to think that they may be
liked when they are read, and it is my hope that they
will serve a good purpose to the historian, in the distant
future, by helping to show that certain fine spirits of
our age were not unappreciated in their own generation.

W. W.

FORT HILL, NEW BRIGHTON,
  STATEN ISLAND, N. Y.,
    September 24, 1898.

3

NEW-YORK

FOUNDED IN

MDCCCLXXXV

THE DUNLAP SOCIETY

# I

# DRAMATIC SPEECHES

# HENRY IRVING

# A WREATH OF LAUREL

## Henry Irving and the Drama.

SPEECH AND POEM AT A FESTIVAL IN HONOR OF
HENRY IRVING, GIVEN BY THE PEN AND
PENCIL CLUB, AT THE WATERLOO HOTEL,
EDINBURGH, OCTOBER 31, 1894.[1]

MR. PRESIDENT AND GENTLEMEN OF
THE PEN AND PENCIL CLUB:

IT is a pleasure and a privilege to meet this distinguished assemblage, the choice and master
spirits of art and of thought in this beautiful and re-
nowned city of Edinburgh,— " dear for her reputation
through the world ": yet the pleasure is not un-
tempered with solicitude. I am deeply conscious of
the honor conferred on me,— a stranger and a wanderer from a distant land,— by your wish that I should
respond to the toast of the Drama, with which my

---

[1] A festival in honor of Henry Irving was given at midnight of October 31,
1894, at the Waterloo Hotel, Edinburgh, by the Pen and Pencil Club, of that
city. About one hundred and fifty persons were present, representative of the
art, literature, and society of Edinburgh. The place was the great hall of the
Waterloo, which thirty years ago was a theatre. The chair was taken by G. W.
W. Barclay, Esq., of Aberdeen,— the vice-chairmen being Messrs. J. C. Dibdin
(grandson of Charles Dibdin, author of the sea songs) and A. W. Vokes.

4

name has been so graciously coupled, and I thank
you, most gratefully, for the signal kindness with which
the mention of that name has been received. The
Drama is an institution with which I have been associated during most of my life, and one which I have, in
an humble way, faithfully labored to serve : yet I cannot fail to reflect that every thought which is likely to
occur to my mind, in speaking to such an audience as
this,— an audience of artists and thinkers,— upon any
subject connected with art, probably has occurred to
each one of my listeners, over and over again.   Under circumstances less important I might venture to
take refuge among the anecdotes.   There is "snug
lying in the abbey" of old Joe Miller.   Under the
circumstances that exist I cannot but remember how
dangerous it is to rehearse old stories in the presence
of club men and experienced men of the world.   The
most felicitous of comic yarns, marred by publicity,
becomes at last monotonous,— like Charles Lamb's
" Poor Relation,"— and " the guests think they have
seen him before."

This moment, for me, accordingly, is one of serious
trial, and I must be permitted to add that my perplex-
ity is heightened by a deep and stirring sense of my

The chairman, referring to the occasion as the twentieth anniversary of Irving's
performance of Hamlet, at the London Lyceum,— then managed by H. L.
Bateman,— paid an earnest tribute to the genius of the actor, and to his wise
and fine conduct of his dramatic career.   Irving, in the course of an eloquent
reply, advocated the establishment of a municipal theatre.   Musical exercises
followed, and speeches were made by Messrs. G. A. Peacock, Bram Stoker,
and J. C. Dibdin.   In reply to the toast of the Drama, I delivered the following
speech and poem.   Much of the speech was humorous, but that part of it was
not reported and has been lost.

extraordinary environment.  Amid the scenes and
associations that now surround me, it is, I think, ex-
ceedingly difficult to fix the mind upon the facts of
the present, or to put into intelligible form the impres-
sions that are prompted by the passing hour.  You, to
whom these scenes are familiar, are able to dwell
among them with comparative composure,— for they
are a part of your every-day experience.  The stranger,
when he looks upon Edinburgh Castle and Holyrood
Palace, the hallowed Greyfriars and the storied Cathedral, the pathetic desolation of Craigmillar and the
royal glory of Dunfermline, is agitated, astonished,
bewildered, and overwhelmed.  There, almost within
the sound of my voice, is the grave of David Hume,
— that strong and splendid historian, that wise philosopher, that benign, pure spirit, whom to remember
is to bless!  In yonder valley, hard by the dust of
Adam Smith and Dugald Stewart, stands the stone
that your national poet, Robert Burns, placed to commemorate the genius of the lamented Ferguson.  At
the foot of your Castle Rock rest the ashes of the wonderful De Quincey.  Along your High Street, tranquil and fearless, going proudly to his death, still
moves, in the gaze of fancy, the imperial figure of the
great Montrose; and through the West Port and
down the hill, while the drums crash and the trumpets
blare, the intrepid Marquis of Dundee rides forth, un-
knowing, to meet his doom.  There is no limit to the
wonderful and inspiring associations of this regal capi-
tal.  I cannot look upon them unmoved.  I should
be grieved indeed if I could walk the streets of your

august and lovely city without a thrill of more than
common joy and gratitude to find myself treading in
the footprints of Walter Scott. Familiar things, I
say, these are to you, whose lot has been cast among
them : but for the stranger it is no common experience
to look upon the home of that illustrious genius whose
influence upon this world, to exalt the human race
and to bless. it, goes hand in hand with that of Shakespeare, and is scarcely second to that of the incomparable master, in the magic and the grace of romantic
art.

In discussing the Drama there is always the danger
— and I do not think it is always avoided — of run-
ning into platitude. Speakers on the Drama are but
too apt to tell us of its decline from certain "palmy
days,"— which no one of them can remember,— and
of the great necessity which exists for "the elevation of
the stage." Nothing could be more false, nothing
more wearisome. The Drama requires neither res-
toration nor authority; for it is one of the elemental
necessities of social life. But, while it stands in no
need of regeneration, it requires, and it ought at all
times to receive, wise and just treatment. In Great
Britain it still endures the odium of conventional prejudice. Dr. Johnson, I believe,— or was it some other
sage ? — observed that a man may brew and still be a
gentleman, while no man can be a gentleman and
bake. The brewer, the tradesman, can go to Court.
The actor is, practically, proscribed—and he is proscribed because of his profession. In America no
such prejudice prevails. There is, of course, the re-

ligious antipathy; but that is dying away. In both
America and Great Britain, however, the stage suffers
under pernicious influences. In both countries there
are vacuous persons who declare that all they want in
the theatre is something to laugh at. In both countries there is a narrow criticism that examines ideals
and emotions with a tape-measure and a microscope.
And in both there is the speculative theatrical manager
who will present anything, no matter how vile, so that
he can draw a good house. We are all familiar with
the specious doctrine that the way to prosper is to
" give the people what they want." I would not be a
fanatic in my enthusiasm for the Drama. I would
not insist upon continual Shakespeare or everlasting
classics. I would not sequester the stage from the
people: but I would most strongly insist that the
Theatre shall not be mobbled up with the Music Hall,
and that intellectual purpose and authority shall control it, and not the crude taste of an idle multitude;—
to the end that prosperity may no longer be possible
to those enemies of art and of society who are willing
to traffic in human weakness and folly.

Something might be said in protest against those
dramatists of the hour who think it well to celebrate
the infatuation of a male fool for a female idiot,— forever ringing the changes upon the ethics of matrimo-
nial incontinence, and upon the vicious triviality of
that profligate living so well designated by Dr. Johnson as " conduct which, in all ages, the good have con-
demned as vicious, and the bad have despised as
foolish." That is a sad abuse. Let us look upon

our Drama not with despondency, but with faith and hope. The children of the gods do not perish. In each successive period of dramatic history a great man has arisen, to bear the torch of genius and to light the pathway of art. In Shakespeare's time it was Burbage. After him came Betterton, Garrick, Kemble, Kean, Macready, and Edwin Booth. To-day the leader is your honored guest, Henry Irving. I need not dwell upon his career. The underlying principles of it are known to all the world,— profound faith in the beauty, purity, and power of dramatic art, and inflexible devotion to a noble ideal of life. This great actor is happily with you, and I know that your lives are brighter for his presence, and that the only touch of sadness in this hour is a thought of the parting that soon must come. Let me conclude these remarks with a few verses of mine,— written to honor him on an earlier occasion, but, perhaps, not inappropriate here,— as at least indicative of what we all feel, not only for him, but for that great actress and beautiful woman Ellen Terry, whose genius and whose superlative charm have potently aided and cheered his progress, and have shed an imperishable splendor upon the artistic achievements of his bright career.

### HENRY IRVING.[1]

. . . . . .

But let the golden waves leap up
 While yet our hearts beat near him!
No bitter drop be in the cup
 With which our hope would cheer him!
Pour the red roses at his feet!
 Wave laurel boughs above him!
And if we part or if we meet
 Be glad and proud to love him!

His life has made this iron age
 More grand and fair in story;
Illumed our Shakespeare's sacred page
 With new and deathless glory;
Refreshed the love of noble fame
 In hearts all sadly faring,
And lit anew the dying flame
 Of genius and of daring.

Long may his radiant summer smile
 Where Albion's rose is dreaming,
And over art's Hesperian isle
 His royal banner streaming;
While every trumpet blast that rolls
 From Britain's lips to hail him
Is echoed in our kindred souls,
 Whose truth can never fail him.

On your white wings, ye angel years,
 Through roseate sunshine springing,
Waft fortune from all happier spheres,
 With garlands and with singing;
Make strong that tender heart and true —
 That thought of Heaven to guide him —
And blessings pour like diamond dew,
 On her that walks beside him!

[1] Copyright by the Macmillan Company, of New York.

And when is said the last farewell,
  So solemn and so certain,
And fate shall strike the prompter's bell
  To drop the final curtain,
Be his, whom every muse hath blest,
  That best of earthly closes—
To sink to rest on England's breast
And sleep beneath her roses.

An earlier tribute of mine to Henry Irving may appropriately be preserved in this place,—a speech and poem, delivered at a festival in his honor, given by many citizens of New York, at Delmonico's, April 6, 1885.

In this illustrious presence and in this memorable hour I do not presume to think that any words of mine are needed to complete the expression of your sense of intellectual obligation to Henry Irving, or your sorrow in bidding him farewell. Having, in other places, said and written much in celebration of this theme, I might well be content to remain silent now. Such, however, was not the will of the immediate managers of this occasion, who lately signified to me that a few words from my lips would be expected here to-night, by way of a God-speed to the parting guest.

Those words I could not decline to speak; and perhaps it is not altogether inappropriate that a voice which has accompanied and proclaimed every one of his great professional triumphs upon the American stage should be heard here, for one moment, in this crowning commemoration of his renown. This hour belongs to friendship. The memories of a long period come thronging into my thoughts; and with them comes that mournful sense of separation which is present to you all.

In every true votary of the dramatic art you will perceive a peculiar and delicate sensibility. This is largely resultant from the fact that an actor, in presenting his art upon the stage, presents also his physical personality — addressing the public as an actual individual, and not through the protective medium of print, or paint, or marble, or other material substance. And just as there is acute sensibility in the artist, so there should be, and naturally and usually there is, a deep sympathy in the nature of the rightful and competent judge of art.

When you have long and patiently studied an actor's intellectual constitution; when you have tried to fathom the depth of his feelings; when you have minutely traced and interpreted the beauty and the mystery of his acting; when, striving to live in his grand ideals of imaginative life, you have been made to live a more exalted and glorious life of your own, it is inevitable that you should become bound to him by ties of an affection as true, as deep, as strong, and as permanent as any that human nature can feel. For this reason you are clustered to-night around this great actor, to bid him Farewell; and I shall be glad if these simple lines of mine can even hint the tenderness which is warm at your hearts:

5

## VALE.[1]

### I.

Now fades across the glimmering deep, now darkly drifts away
The royal monarch of our hearts, the glory of our day:
The pale stars shine, the night wind sighs, the sad sea makes its
  moan,
And we, bereft, are standing here, in silence and alone.


Gone every shape of power and dread his magic touch could paint:
Gone haunted Aram's spectral face, and England's martyred saint:
Gone Mathias, of the frenzied soul, and Louis' sceptred guile,
The gentle head of poor Lesurques, and Hamlet's holy smile.


No more in gray Messina's halls shall love and revel twine;
No more on Portia's midnight bowers the moon of summer
  shine;
No golden barge on Hampton's stream salute the perfum'd
  shore;
No ghost on Denmark's rampart cliff affright our pulses more.


The morning star of art, he rose across the eastern sea,
To wake the slumbering harp and set the frozen fountain free:
Now, wrapt in glory's mist, he seeks his orient skies again,
And tender thoughts in sorrowing hearts are all that must re-
  main.


### II.

Slow fade, across a drearier sea, beneath a darker sky,
The dreams that cheer, the lights that lure, the baffled hopes that
  die.
Youth's trust, Love's bliss, Ambition's pride — the white wings
  all are flown,
And Memory walks the lonely shore, indifferent and alone.

Yet sometimes o'er that shadowy deep, by wand'ring breezes
    blown,
Float odors from Hesperian isles, with music's organ tone,
And something stirs within the breast, a secret, nameless thrill,
To say, though worn and sear and sad, our hearts are human
    still;—

If not the torrid diamond wave that made young life sublime,
If not the tropic rose that bloomed in every track of time,
If not exultant passion's glow when all the world was fair,
At least one flash of heaven, one breath of art's immortal air!


Ah, God make bright, for many a year, on Beauty's heavenly
    shrine,
This hallowed fire that Thou hast lit, this sacred soul of Thine,
While Love's sweet light and Sorrow's tear — life's sunshine
    dimm'd with showers —
Shall keep for aye his memory green in these true hearts of
    ours!

# IAN MACLAREN

yours faithfully
Ian MacLaren

# Ian Maclaren.

## POETRY AND PATHOS IN SCOTTISH LITERATURE.

SPEECH AND POEM AT A LOTOS CLUB DINNER
TO IAN MACLAREN (REV. JOHN WATSON, D. D.),
NEW YORK, DECEMBER 6, 1896.

MR. PRESIDENT AND GENTLEMEN OF THE LOTOS CLUB:

IT is a pleasure to know, from the assurance we have just received, that every man who rises upon the platform of the Lotos Club immediately becomes eloquent,— for I do not recall an occasion when the need of eloquence was more urgent. In this distinguished presence I should have been pleased to remain silent ; to listen, not to speak. But since, in your kindness, you will have it otherwise, I must thank you as well as I can, and I do thank you, most sincerely, for the privilege of participating in your whole-hearted and lovely tribute to the great writer who is your guest to-night. All that I feel, as an humble and obscure votary of literature standing in the presence of one of its masters, could not be briefly spoken, but the little that it seems essential I should say can be said in a few words. My oratorical ministrations, as many of my present hearers are aware, have usually, and almost exclusively, been invoked upon occasions of farewell,— until I have

15

come to feel like that serious Boston clergyman who
declined to read the wedding service because he considered himself "reserved for funerals." A certain
delightful humorist now present, however, has recorded
for you the reassuring opinion of the grave-digger of
Drumtochty, that there is no real pleasure in a marriage, because you never know how it will end:
whereas there is no risk whatever in a burial. Under
these circumstances you know what to expect. It is
no part of my intention to infringe upon the facetious
treatment of this occasion.

About eight years ago, when I visited for the first
time [1888], the glorious city of Edinburgh, I had the
singular good fortune to meet with a venerable gentleman,—Capt. W. Sandylands,—then more than eighty,
who, in his youth, had personally known Sir Walter
Scott; and he described, minutely and with natural enthusiasm, the appearance of that great man, as he had
often seen him, when walking in Prince's street, on
his way to and from that Castle street house which
has become a shrine of devout pilgrimage from every
quarter of the world. What a privilege it was to have
looked upon that astonishing genius — that splendid
image of chivalry and heroism! To have heard his
voice! To have seen his greeting smile! To have
clasped the hand that wrote "Ivanhoe" and "The
Antiquary," "Old Mortality" and "The Lady of the
Lake"! As I listened, I felt myself drawn nearer
and ever nearer to the sacred presence of a great
benefactor; to the presence of that wonderful man,
who, next to Shakespeare, has, during all my life, been

to me the most bountiful giver of cheer and strength
and hope and happy hours. To you, my hearers, fortunate children of the Lotos flower, within the twenty-
six years of your club life, has fallen the golden opportunity of personal communion with some of the
foremost men, whether of action or of thought, who
have arisen to guide and illumine the age;—Froude,
who so royally depicted the pageantry and pathos of
the Past; Grant, who so superbly led the warrior le-
gions of the Present; Charles Kingsley, with his deep
and touching voice of humanity; Wilkie Collins, with
his magic wand of mystery and his weird note of romance; Oliver Wendell Holmes, the modern Theoc-
ritus, the most comforting of philosophers; Mark Twain,
true and tender heart and first humorist of the age;
and Henry Irving, noble gentleman and prince of
actors. Those bright names, and many more, will rise
in your glad remembrance; and I know you will agree
that, in every case, when the generous mind pays its
homage to the worth of a great man, the impulse is
not that of adulation, but that of gratitude. Such is
the feeling of this hour, when now you are assembled
to honor the author of the " Bonnie Brier Bush," the
most exquisite literary artist, in the vein of mingled
humor and pathos, who has risen in Scotland, since the
age when Sir Walter Scott,—out of the munificence
of his fertile genius,—created Wamba the Jester, Cud-
die Headrigg, Caleb Balderstone, Dugald Dalgetty,
Dominie Sampson, and Jeannie Deans.

There are two principles of art, or canons of criticism, call them what you will, to which my allegiance

6

is irrevocably plighted: that it is always best to show
to mankind the things which are to be emulated,
rather than the things which are to be shunned, and
(since the moral element, whether as morality or im-
morality, is present in all things, perpetually obvious,
and always able to take care of itself), that no work
of art should have an avowed moral. Those principles are conspicuously illustrated in the writings of
Dr. Watson. Without didacticism they teach, and
without effort they charm. Their strength is elemental; their stroke is no less swift than sure,—like
the scimetar of Saladdin, which, with one sudden waft
of the strong and skilful hand, could shear in twain the
scarf of silk or the cushion of down. Dr. Watson has
himself told you that "we cannot analyze a spiritual
fact." We all know that the spirit of his art is noble,
and that its influence is tender and sweet. We all
know that it has, again and again, suddenly, and at
the same instant, brought the smile to our lips and the
tears into our eyes. I cannot designate its secret. I
suppose it to be the same inaccessible charm of truth
that hallows the simple words of the dying Lear:

> Pray you undo this button: Thank you, sir;

the same ineffable pathos that is in the death speech
of Brutus:

> Night hangs upon mine eyes; my bones would rest,
> That have but labour'd to attain this hour;

the same voice of patient grief that breathes in the
touching farewell of Cassius:

> Time is come round,
> And where I did begin there shall I end —
> My life is run his compass;

the same woful sense and utterance of human misery that thrills through the wonderful words of Timon:

> My long sickness
> Of health and living now begins to mend,
> And nothing brings me all things;

the same exquisite flow of feeling that is in the lilt of Burns, when he sings of the Jacobite cavalier:

> He turned him right and round about
> Upon the Irish shore;
> And gave his bridle reins a shake
> With adieu for evermore, my dear,
> And adieu for evermore.

I remember that magic touch in some of the poems of Richard Henry Stoddard, and in some of the stories — the matchless American stories — of Bret Harte. I recognize it in the sad talk of poor old Bows, the fiddler, when, in the night, upon the bridge at Chatteris, he speaks to the infatuated Pendennis, about the heartless and brainless actress to whom they both are devoted, and drops the stump of his cigar into the dark water below. I feel it in that solemn moment when, as the tolling bell of the Charterhouse chapel calls him for the last time to prayer, the finest gentleman in all fiction answers to his name and stands in the presence of the Master: and I say that there is but one step from the death-bed of Colonel Newcome to the death-bed of William Maclure.

Through all that is finest and most precious in literature, like the King's Yarn in the cables of the old British navy, runs that lovely note of poetry and pathos. So, from age to age, the never-dying torch of genius is passed from hand to hand. When Robert Burns died, in 1796, it might have been thought that the authentic voice of poetry had been hushed forever; but, even then, a boy was playing on the banks of the Dee, whose song of passion and of grief would one day convulse the world; and the name of him was Byron. In that year of fatality, 1832, when Crabbe and Scott and Goethe died, and when the observer could not but remember that Keats and Shelley and Byron were also gone, it might again have been thought that genius had taken its final flight to Heaven; but, even then, among the pleasant plains of Lincolnshire, the young Tennyson was ripening for the glory that was to come. And now, when we look around us, and see, in England, such writers as Blackmore, Thomas Hardy, and Rudyard Kipling, and, in Scotland, such writers as John Watson, and Barrie, and William Black, and Crockett, I think that we may feel,— much as we reverence the genius of Dickens and Thackeray and George Eliot, and much as we deplore their loss,— that the time of acute mourning for those great leaders has come to an end.

Nor am I surprised that the present awakening of poetry, passion, and pathos in literature has come from Scotland. When, on a windy Sabbath day of cloud and sunshine, I have stood upon the old Calton hill, and, under a blue and black sky, seen the white smoke from a thousand chimneys drifting over the gray city of Edinburgh; when from the breezy, fragrant Braid Hills I have gazed out over the crystal Forth, "whose islands on its bosom lie, like emeralds chased with gold"; when from the gloomy height of the Necropolis I have looked across to ancient Glasgow and the gaunt and grim Cathedral of Rob Roy; when I have seen Dumbarton rock burst through the mountainous mist and frown upon the sparkling Clyde; when, from the slopes of Ben Cruachan, I have watched the sunset shadows darkening in the dim valleys of Glen Strae; when, just before the dawn, I have paused beside the haunted Cona, and looked up at the cold stars watching over the black chasms of Glencoe; and when at midnight, I have stood alone in the broken and ruined Cathedral of Iona, and heard only the ghostly fluttering of the rooks and the murmuring surges of the desolate sea, I have not wondered that Scotland has all the poetry, and that deep in the heart of every true Scotchman there is a chord that trembles not alone to the immortal melodies of Burns and Scott, but to the eternal harmonies of Nature and of God. There may be countries that are more romantic and more poetical. I have not seen them; and as I think of Scotland I echo the beautiful words of Burns:

> Still o'er the scene my mem'ry wakes,
>     And fondly broods with miser care;
> Time but th' impression deeper makes,
>     As streams their channels deeper wear.

I propose this sentiment: Scotland, its glories, its memories, its beauties, and its loves: and I will close this address with some verses of mine, expressive of the feeling with which I parted from the most sacred of Scottish shrines:

### FAREWELL TO IONA.[1]

#### I.

Shrined among their crystal seas —
Thus I saw the Hebrides:

All the land with verdure dight;
All the heavens flushed with light;

Purple jewels 'neath the tide;
Hill and meadow glorified;

Beasts at ease and birds in air;
Life and beauty everywhere!

Shrined amid their crystal seas —
Thus I saw the Hebrides.

#### II.

Fading in the sunset smile —
Thus I left the Holy Isle;

Saw it slowly fade away,
Through the mist of parting day;

Saw its ruins, grim and old,
And its bastions, bathed in gold,

[1] Copyright by the Macmillan Company, of New York.

Rifted crag and snowy beach,
Where the sea-gulls swoop and screech,

Vanish, and the shadows fall,
To the lonely curlew's call.

Fading in the sunset smile —
Thus I left the Holy Isle.


### III.

As Columba, old and ill,
Mounted on the sacred hill,

Raising hands of faith and prayer,
Breathed his benediction there,—

Stricken with its solemn grace —
Thus my spirit blessed the place:

O'er it while the ages range,
Time be blind and work no change!

On its plenty be increase!
On its homes perpetual peace!

While around its lonely shore
Wild winds rave and breakers roar,

Round its blazing hearths be blent
Virtue, comfort, and content!

On its beauty, passing all,
Ne'er may blight nor shadow fall!

Ne'er may vandal foot intrude
On its sacred solitude!

May its ancient fame remain
Glorious, and without a stain;

And the hope that ne'er departs,
Live within its loving hearts!


IV.

Slowly fades the sunset light,
Slowly round me falls the night:

Gone the Isle, and distant far
All its loves and glories are;

Yet forever, in my mind,
Still will sigh the wand'ring wind,

And the music of the seas,
Mid the lonely Hebrides.

# MY LOTOS NIGHT

" AND WHAT HAVE I TO GIVE YOU BACK, WHOSE WORTH
MAY COUNTERPOISE THIS RICH AND PRECIOUS GIFT ? "

— SHAKESPEARE

# The Stage and its Apostles.

SPEECH AND POEM DELIVERED BEFORE THE LOTOS
CLUB, NEW YORK, AT A FESTIVAL IN HONOR
OF THE SPEAKER, APRIL 24, 1897.

MR. PRESIDENT AND GENTLEMEN
OF THE LOTOS CLUB:

THE meaning and the elements of this charming
spectacle,—the lights, the flowers, the music, the
gentle, eager, friendly faces, the kind and generous
words which have been so graciously spoken, the cordial sympathy and welcome with which those words
have been received, the many denotements, unequivocal and decisive, of personal good will,—are as
touching to the heart as they are lovely to the senses,
and a fond and proud remembrance of this beautiful
scene will abide with me as long as anything in my
life is remembered.

On previous occasions when I have been privileged
to participate in festivals of the Lotos Club it has been
my glad province to unite in homage to others: on
the present occasion I am to thank you,—and I do
thank you, most heartily,—for a tribute of friendship
to myself. Gratitude is easy; but an adequate expression of it, under the circumstances which exist, is
well nigh impossible. The Moslems have a fanciful

27

belief that the soul of the Faithful, just before it enters into Paradise, must walk, barefooted, across a bridge of red-hot iron. That ordeal not inaptly typifies the experience of the honored guest who, at a feast like this, is bidden to consider his merits, must hear the commendation of his deeds, and must utter his thanks for the bounty of praise. My first impulse would be to declare that I have done nothing to merit this honor : but, without qualification, to disclaim all desert would be to impugn your judgment and discredit your kindness. The great and wise Dr. Johnson, I remember, did not scruple to accept the praises of his sovereign. " When the King had said it," he afterward remarked, " it was to be so." My literary life,— dating from the publication of my first book, in Boston, in 1854,— has extended over a period of forty-three years, thirty-seven of which have been passed, in active labor, in this community. Since 1865 I have been the accredited and responsible representative of " The New York Tribune " in the department of the Drama. In the dramatic field, and also in the fields of Poetry, Essay, Biography and Travel, I have put forth my endeavors, striving to add something of permanent value to the literature of my native land. No one knows so well as I do my failures and my defects. But,— I have tried to follow the right course; I have done my best; and now, in the review of that long period of labor, if you, my friends, find anything that is worthy of approval, anything that seems, in your eyes, to justify such a testimonial as this, it would ill become me to repel an approbation which it is honorable to possess, and which

I have labored and hoped to deserve. When the King has said it, it is to be so!

While, however, I gratefully accept and deeply value the honor that you have bestowed, I feel that you have intended something much more important and significant than a compliment to me. You have desired to effect a rally of stage veterans and of the friends of the stage, and, at a time of theatrical depression, when the fortunes of the actor seem dubious and perplexed, to evince, once more, your practical admiration for the great art of acting, your high esteem for the stage as a means of social welfare, and your sympathy with every intellectual force that is arrayed for its support. The drift of your thought, therefore, naturally, is toward a consideration of the relation between the theatre and society, together with the province of those writers by whom that relation is habitually discussed. It is a wide subject, and one upon which there are many and sharply contrasted views. For my own part, I have always believed — of all the arts — that they are divinely commissioned to lead humanity, and not to follow it, and that it is the supreme duty of a writer to advocate, and to exercise, a noble influence, rather than much to concern himself with the delivery of expert opinions upon individual achievement. The right principle is expressed in the quaint words of Emerson:

> I hold it a little matter
> Whether your jewel be of pure water,
> A rose diamond or a white,
> But whether it dazzle me with light.

The essential thing is the inspiration that is fluent from a great personality. The passport to momentous and permanent victory, whether on the stage or off, is the salutary and ennobling strength of splendid character. It is not enough that you possess ability; your ability must mean something to others, and the world must be exalted by it.

Many images crowd upon the mind at such a moment as this, and many names are remembered which it would be good to mention and pleasant to hear. My thoughts go back to my young acquaintance with such stage advocates as Epes Sargent and Edwin Percy Whipple, Henry Giles and William Clapp, Wallace Thaxter and Charles T. Congdon, Francis A. Durivage, Charles Fairbanks, Curtis Guild, and James Oakes (the friend of Forrest); and, as I think of them, I recall a time when Catherine Farren was the Juliet of my dreams, and Julia Dean the goddess of every youth's idolatry, and when the green curtain (in those days it was always green), never rose except upon a land of enchantment, and the roses were always bright by the calm Bendemeer. Much might be said of those old times, and much might be said of the critical art, as it was exemplified by those old writers. But this is not the moment for either a memoir or an essay; and, after all, experience may sometimes utter in a sentence the lesson of a life. As I have said elsewhere,— to understand human nature; to absorb and coördinate the literature of the drama; to see the mental, moral, and spiritual aspect of the stage, and likewise to see the popular aspect of

it; to write for a public of miscellaneous readers, and
at the same time to respect the feelings and interpret
the ambitions of actors; to praise with discretion and
yet with force; to censure without asperity; to think
quickly and speak quickly, and yet avoid error; to oppose sordid selfishness, which forever strives to degrade
every high ideal; to give not alone knowledge, study,
and technical skill, but the best powers of the mind
and the deepest feelings of the heart to the embellish-
ment of the art of others, and to do that with an art
of your own,— this it is to accomplish the work of the
dramatic reviewer. It is a work of serious moment
and incessant difficulty. But it has its bright side;
for, as years speed on and life grows bleak and lone-
some, it is the Stage that gives relief from paltry con-
ventionality; it is the Stage, with its sunshine of humor and its glory of imagination, that wiles us away
from our defeated ambitions, our waning fortunes, and
the broken idols of our vanishing youth. In the long
process of social development,— at least within the last
three hundred years,— no other single force has borne
a more conspicuous or a more potential part. " The
reason of things," said Dr. South, "lies in a small compass, if a man could but find it out." The reason of
the Drama has never been a mystery. All life has, for its
ultimate object, a spiritual triumph. The Divine Spirit
works in humanity by many subtle ways. It is man's
instinctive, intuitive imitation of nature that creates ar-
tificial objects of beauty. Those, in turn, react upon
the human mind and deepen and heighten its sense of
the beautiful. It is man's interpretation of humanity

that has revealed to him his Divine Father and his spiritual destiny. All things work together for that result,— the dramatic art deeply and directly, because, when rightly administered, it is the pure mirror of all that is glorious in character and all that is noble and gentle in the conduct of life; showing ever the excellence to be emulated and the glory to be gained, soothing our cares, dispelling our troubles, and casting the glamour of romantic grace upon all the common-places of the world. What happy dreams it has inspired! What grand ideals it has imparted! With what gentle friendships it has blessed and beautified our lives!

Moralists upon the Drama are fond of dwelling on its alleged decline from certain "palmy days" of the past,— a vague period which no one distinctly remembers or defines, and which still recedes, the more diligently it is pursued, "in the dark backward and abysm of time." One difference between the Past and the Present is that the stage which once lived in a camp now lives in a palace. Another difference is that eminent talents which once were concentrated are now diffused. The standard of taste has fluctuated. At the beginning of the century it appears to have been more fastidious and more intellectual than it is now, but not more so than it has two or three times been, within the intervening period. In my boyhood the great tragic genius of the stage was the elder Booth, whom I saw as Pescara, during his last engagement in Boston, in 1851,— and a magnificent image he was, of appalling power and terror. The popular sovereign,

however, was Edwin Forrest, and for many years his
influence survived, affecting the style of such com-
peers as Eddy, Neafie, Scott, Proctor, Kirby, and Mar-
shall, and more or less moulding that of the romantic
Edwin Adams, the intellectual Lawrence Barrett, and
the gentle, generous, affectionate, stalwart John Mc-
Cullough, " the noblest Roman of them all." In comedy the prevalent tradition was that of Finn,— whom
I never saw, but of whom I constantly heard,— but
the actual prince was the elder Wallack ; and very soon
after he had sparkled into splendid popularity the rosy
gods of mirth released such messengers of happiness as
Warren and Gilbert, Burton and Blake, Hackett and
Fisher, Placide and Owens, and the buoyant John
Brougham, whose memory is still cherished in all our
hearts. A little later,— the more intellectual taste in
tragedy gaining a sudden preëminence, from the reac-
tion against Forrest,— the spiritual beauty and the wild
and thrilling genius of Edwin Booth enchanted the
public mind and captured an absolute sovereignty of
the serious stage ; while, in comedy, the glittering figure
of Lester Wallack bore to the front rank, and reared
more splendidly than ever before, the standard of
Wilks, and Lewis, and Elliston, which had been preserved and transmitted by Charles Kemble, the elder
Wallack, and both the chieftains of the house of
Mathews. Meanwhile Murdock, Vandenhoff, E. L.
Davenport, and the younger James Wallack maintained, in royal state, the fine classic tradition of
Kemble, Cooper, Macready, and Young; the grandeur of Sarah Siddons lived again in Charlotte Cush-
8

man; and, in the realm of imaginative, romantic, human drama, a more exquisite artist of humor and of tears than ever yet had risen on our stage — an artist who is to Acting what Reynolds was to Painting and what Hood was to Poetry — carried natural portraiture to ideal perfection, and made illustrious the name of Joseph Jefferson.

The stage, in itself, is not degenerate. The old fires are not yet dead. The world moves onward, and "the palmy days" move onward with the world. At this moment the public taste is fickle and the public morality infirm; but this moment is reactionary, and of course it will not last. The stage has been degraded; the press has been polluted; the church has been shaken; the whole fabric of society has been threatened. The assaults of materialism, blighting faith and discrediting romance, have had a temporary triumph. The dangerous delusion that there is a divinity in the untaught multitude has everywhere promoted disorder, violence, and vulgarity. So, from time to time, the dregs endeavor to reach the top. But all this fever and turmoil will pass; and, in those saner times which are at hand, the Stage, as we know it and love it,— the stage of Wignell and Dunlap, the stage of Keach and Barry, the stage of Wallack, and Booth, and Henry Irving, and Augustin Daly, the stage that, in our day, has been adorned by Rachel, Ristori, Seebach, Janauschek, and Modjeska, and by Adelai Neilson and Mary Anderson (twin stars of loveliness, the one all passion and sorrow, the other all innocence, light, and joy!), the stage that possesses the wild, poetic beauty and rare, elusive, celestial spirit of Ellen Terry, and the enchanting womanhood and blithe, gleeful, tender human charm of Ada Rehan, the stage that is consecrated to intellect, genius and beauty,— will again assert its splendid power, and will again rejoice in all the honors, and manifest all the inherent virtues, of the stage of our forefathers, in the best of their golden days.

But I detain you too long from voices more eloquent than mine, and thoughts more worthy. There is little more to be said. My career as an active writer about the stage may, perhaps, be drawing to a close. It has covered the period of more than one generation; it has been freighted with exacting responsibility; it has been inexpressibly laborious; and its conclusion would cause me no regret. I have no enmities, and if ever in my life I have wounded any heart, I have done so without intention, and I hope that my error may be forgiven. For the rest, I should exactly express my feelings, if I might venture to use the words of Landor:

> I strove with none, for none was worth my strife;
>   Nature I loved, and next to Nature, Art;
> I warmed both hands against the fire of life:
>   It sinks, and I am ready to depart.

Let me close this response with some lines that I have written, remembering other days and other faces, now hidden behind the veil, and remembering that for me also the curtain soon may fall:

## MEMORY.[1]

### I.

A tangled garden, bleak and dry
And silent 'neath a dark'ning sky,
Is all that barren Age retains
Of costly Youth's superb domains.
Mute in its bosom, cold and lone,
A dial watches, on a stone ;
The vines are sere, the haggard boughs
In dusky torpor dream and drowse ;
The paths are deep with yellow leaves,
In which the wind of evening grieves ;
And up and down, and to and fro,
One pale gray shadow wanders slow.

### II.

When now the fading sunset gleams
Across a glimm'ring waste of dreams ;
When now the shadows eastward fall,
And twilight hears the curlew's call ;
When blighted now the lily shows,
And no more bloom is on the rose ;
What phantom of the dying day
Shall gild the wanderer's sombre way —
What new illusion of delight —
What magic, ushering in the night ?
For, deep beneath the proudest will
The heart must have its solace still.

### III.

Ah, many a hope too sweet to last
Is in that garden of the Past,
And many a flower that once was fair
Lies cold and dead and wither'd there;

1 Copyright by the Macmillan Company, of New York.

Youth's promise, trusted Friendship's bliss,
Fame's laurel, Love's enraptured kiss,
Beauty and strength — the spirit's wings —
And the glad sense of natural things,
And times that smile, and times that weep —
All shrouded in the cells of sleep;
While o'er them careless zephyrs pass,
And sunbeams, in the rustling grass.

IV.

So ends it all : but never yet
Could the true heart of love forget,
And grander sway was never known
Than his who reigns on Memory's throne!
Though grim the threat and dark the frown
With which the pall of night comes down,
Though all the scene be drear and wild,
Life once was precious, once it smiled,
And in his dream he lives again
With ev'ry joy that crowned it then,
And no remorse of time can dim
The splendor of the Past for him !

V.

The sea that round his childhood played
Still makes the music once it made,
And still in Fancy's chambers sing
The breezes of eternal Spring ;
While, thronging Youth's resplendent track,
The princes and the queens come back,
And everywhere the dreary mould
Breaks into Nature's green and gold!
It is not night — or, if it be,
So let the night descend for me,
When Mem'ry's radiant dream shall cease,
Slow lapsing into perfect peace.

# ACTING AND WRITING

# The Intellectual Standard in Acting and Writing.

SPEECH DELIVERED BEFORE THE ACTORS' FUND SOCIETY, AT THE GARRICK THEATRE, NEW YORK, JUNE 8, 1897.

MR. PRESIDENT AND LADIES AND GENTLEMEN:

IT is an honor and a pleasure to be permitted to participate in this festival of art, taste, scholarship and friendship, within the limits of the dramatic profession, and I thank you for the kindness with which my name has been greeted. After about forty years of continuous public service, as a reviewer of the acted Drama and as an essayist on the art of acting and on the achievements of actors, I hope it will not be considered a presumption if I venture to speak of myself as a friend of the stage. In that capacity I respond, as well as I may, to this summons — in that capacity and that alone.

The fact that an old professional reviewer of the drama is asked to say a word, on this occasion, seems to imply that some among you are mindful of the relation which exists between the stage and its reviewers, and are willing to remember it with kindness, at this time. For my part, I wish that the relation between actor and commentator might always be viewed as one of sympathy, and always remembered with kindness. Upon both sides there are, perhaps, somewhat mistaken views. " All the world's a stage,"— but the stage is not all the world. The press is a power,— but the destiny enwrapt in character is a greater power than the press. Actors sometimes expect too much. Writers sometimes assume both omniscience and omnipotence. A little moderation might promote that fraternal feeling which certainly is desirable between the professors of kindred arts.

Upon the province of the stage it is not needful for me here to expatiate. Upon the province of the press my views are, perhaps, somewhat peculiar. If I were to suggest a line of thought, I should declare that the function of the press is, first, to furnish the news, and, secondly, to comment upon it in such a way as to guide the public taste and opinion toward practical favor of all things which are good. No writer can either make or unmake the reputation of an actor. He may accelerate the success of merit or the failure of vain pretense, but he can neither suppress the one nor sustain the other. Words are powerful, not because they are spoken, but because they are true; and it is in the wise, clear, and cogent exposition of principles that truth makes itself practically felt. Personal praise and personal censure have little, if any, serious effect — for no one regards them. " What harm does it do to a man," said Dr. Johnson, " to call him Holofernes ? " The proper critic for most actors is the stage manager. It is only the exceptional person, in any art, who incarnates those influences which make that art important to society, and thus render it a proper subject of public discussion. Actors ought not to read anything that is printed about themselves, whether it be good, bad, or indifferent. Upon the one hand, printed commendation may prove an incentive to vanity,— which usually needs no encouragement,— while, on the other hand, printed censure is sure to prove a depressing and enervating influence.

Early in my life (I do not speak as an actor, but as a writer), the poet Longfellow, at whose fireside I was often a guest, said to me: " I receive many reviews of my writings. I look at the beginning, and if I find that an article is agreeable, I read it through ; if not, I drop it into my fire, and that is an end of the worry. You are at the beginning of your career. Never read unpleasant criticisms, and never answer an attack." I took that counsel to heart. I have never answered an attack, and it is many years since I have read any reference to myself in print. I have a vague impression that references occur,— sometimes friendly and sometimes hostile,— but I have kept myself in ignorance of almost all of them, and thus I have been able to do my work in comparative peace. My advice to actors has always been to take the same course,— to avoid all reviews, my own included.

Discussion of the stage is intended not for actors, but for readers, and it fulfils its purpose,— almost the only purpose it can fulfil,— when it interests the reader in the subject. Individual actors may sometimes be wounded by an exposition of principles of art: that is almost inevitable : but the greatest service any writer can render to the Drama is to oppose,— at all times and with all his strength,— those influences which tend to degrade its intellectual standards. A few examples will enforce my meaning. About 1861 Charles Fechter appeared upon the English stage and gave an extraordinary performance of Hamlet. It subsequently (1869–70) reached America. It was "the rage" upon both sides of the sea. In a technical sense it was a performance of ability, but it was chiefly remarkable for light hair and bad English. Fanny Kemble tells a story of a lady who, at a dinner in London, was asked by a neighboring guest whether she had seen Mr. Fechter as Hamlet. "No," she said, "I have not; and I think I should not care to hear the English blank verse spoken by a foreigner." The inquirer gazed meditatively upon his plate for some time, and then he said, "But Hamlet *was* a foreigner, was n't he?" That is the gist of the whole matter. We were to have the manner of "nature," in blank verse. We were to have Hamlet in light hair, because Danes are sometimes blonde. We were to have the great soliloquy on life and death omitted, because it stops the action of the play.[1] We were to have the blank verse turned into a foreigner's broken English prose. We were to have Hamlet crossing his legs, upon the gravestone, as if he were Sir Charles Coldstream; and this was to be "nature." Mr. Fechter's plan may have been finely executed, but it was radically wrong, and it could not rightly be accepted.

[1] Mr. Fechter did not discard that soliloquy, but he expressed, to Lester Wallack,— who mentioned it to me,— his opinion that the omission of that passage would be advantageous to the movement of the play; and he always spoke it as if it were prose.

Some courage was required to oppose it, because Mr. Fechter had come to us (to me among others), personally commended by no less a man than the great Charles Dickens.   A little later we had " the blonde" craze.   Horace Greeley once said to me: "Mr. Winter, what is a blonde?   What is it like?"   "Sir," I said, "it is an exuberant young female who has bleached her hair, in order to resemble an albino, and who sings, dances, and prattles nonsense."   A little later came the "Black Crook" craze — the semi-nude figure and the red-fire spectacle.   Those things were not intrinsically injurious.   I have never known sound moral instincts to be corrupted by anything on the stage.   But those forces were injurious to the art of acting and to " the legitimate drama," in which I devotedly believe, and therefore it was right and necessary to oppose them.   A little later came the great Salvini, a man of remarkable powers, of extraordinary physique, of vast experience, and of a colossal reputation. He performed Othello — and he gave a radically wrong performance.   Half of it was grossly animal and sensual, and the other half of it was hideously ferocious.   You cannot find that Moor in the pages of Shakespeare.   It was impossible to resist the power of Salvini's executive dramatic genius; but his standard was radically wrong, for the English classic drama, and therefore it was rightly opposed ; for if the physical method of Salvini be correct, all the traditions of the English stage are useless, and every student of Shakespeare, from Coleridge to Dowden, has gone astray.   Next, out of France, came Sarah Bernhardt, a woman of rare powers and large experience, who, almost invariably, with an iteration not less astonishing than deplorable, devoted her genius to the exposition of the most pernicious and hateful ideal of woman that can be imagined — the woman who is radically depraved, sensual, carnal, and base, and whose loathsome career of appetite and crime culminates in murder and terminates in violent death. The skill with which that ideal was presented impressed many people as marvellous. The effect of it was that of distress, horror, and aversion,— causing the spectator to remember the theatre, not as a temple of beauty, but as a hospital or a madhouse. Latest of all these dramatic "fads" came a series of unfragrant plays, exploiting the relation of the blackguard and the demirep, calling it "a social problem," and causing no better effect than a profound disgust for human nature, together with the domestic embarrassment of awkward questions at breakfast. Other examples might be cited, but these suffice. Opposition to the fancy of the hour may, at the moment, seem unwise and unkind, but, in the long run, it is seen to be right; for the principles of dramatic art do not change; the moral law is inexorable; and the duty of the critic, at all times, is to protect the stage against every wrong and bad influence, and to maintain and insist that acting can achieve the best results, and rise to the highest summits, and still remain within the limits of good breeding and good taste.

It was lately my fortune to be greatly honored by the Lotos Club, of New York, with a complimentary

banquet, the gracious tribute of friendly persons, who
see that Time has showered me with silver, and who,
as they think of many farewells, may perhaps have
reflected that yet another is not far away. As I
looked around upon those crowded tables I could not
but notice that the countenances were mostly those of
strangers; but I saw, as in a vision, the faces of more
than a hundred actors, men and women of the past,
all of whom were my personal friends; all of whom
would gladly have been present; all of whom were
gone! And the tender lines of Uhland floated into
my mind:

> Take, O boatman, thrice thy fee,—
> Take, I give it willingly;
> For, invisible to thee,
> Spirits twain have crossed with me.

What was the peculiarity of those actors of the
Past? Their peculiarity was that, with little exception, they were engaged in doing noble things. They
aimed at splendid intellectual results. Is that the
case, to any considerable extent, upon the American
stage to-day? And if it be not the case to-day, why
should it not be? The same human nature exists.
The sunrise and the sunset are still beautiful. Youth
and innocence and goodness are as much in the world
as they ever were. Art is still subtle; genius is still
sublime; and still the fires of love and hope are burning with immortal splendor on the living altars of the
human heart.

It is said that we cling too much to the Past. Well,
some of us, perhaps, do. It was noticed by Patrick

Henry that "the past at least is secure." What else
have we got, to cling to? The past is the glory of
Greece and of Rome. The past is the splendid
civilization and the matchless literature of England.
The past is Shakespeare, and Milton, and Byron, and
Scott, and Wordsworth, and Burns, and Shelley, and
Coleridge, and Tennyson. The past is Burbage,
and Betterton, and Garrick, and Kemble, and Kean,
and Macready, and Forrest, and Davenport, and
Cushman, and Edwin Booth — and all the rest of that
long line of superb actors by whom your profession
has been ennobled and adorned. And just as we
travel in foreign lands to absorb the beauty that
we would reproduce and perpetuate in our own, so
we love and venerate and study the past, in order, by
its lessons of grandeur and of grace, to advance, to
ennoble, and to consecrate the present.

# THE ANCIENT GLORIES OF THE
# ROMAN CATHOLIC CHURCH

10

# The Ancient Glories of
# The Roman Catholic Church.

SPEECH AND POEM AT A FESTIVAL IN HONOR OF JUDGE
JOSEPH F. DALY, GIVEN BY THE CATHOLIC CLUB,
NEW YORK, NOVEMBER 6, 1897.

MR. PRESIDENT AND GENTLEMEN OF
THE CATHOLIC CLUB:

SPEECH is said to be silver, silence to be golden,
and since I was ever a believer in the gold standard, it would be my preference to remain silent,— to
listen, not to speak. But, since you wish it to be
otherwise, I will say a few words, to thank you for your
kind greeting and for the pleasure of participating in
your festival. It is a festival with which I deeply
sympathize,— because its purpose is to express affection for a beloved comrade, and to pay a tribute of
honor to a noble gentleman. For the privilege of
being present on this occasion I am indebted to no
merit of my own, but to a long-existent friendship
with your distinguished guest,— a friendship which,
beginning thirty years ago, has never known a single
passing cloud, but has grown ever lovelier and more
precious as those years have drifted away. Your kind
invitation, accordingly, came to me more as a com-
mand than a request; and also, let me add, consid-

ering the name and the character of your club, it came
to me with irresistible allurement.

The bond of your society, as I comprehend it, is
not only that of friendship, but that of religion.  Behind the Catholic Club stands the Catholic Church,
and to think of the Catholic Church is to think of the
oldest, the most venerable, and the most powerful institution existing among men.  I am not a churchman,
of any kind: that, possibly, is my misfortune : but I
am conscious of a profound obligation of gratitude to
that wise, august, austere, yet tenderly human ecclesiastical power which, self-centred amid the vicissitudes of human affairs, and provident for men of
learning, imagination, and sensibility throughout the
world, has preserved the literature and art of all the
centuries, has made architecture the living symbol of
celestial aspiration, and, in poetry and in music, has
heard, and has transmitted, the authentic voice of God.
I say that I am not a churchman; but I would also
say that the best hours of my life have been hours of
meditation passed in the  glorious  cathedrals  and
among the sublime ecclesiastical ruins of England.   I
have worshipped in Canterbury and  York; in Winchester and Salisbury; in Lincoln and Durham; in
Ely, and in Wells.   I have stood in Tintern, when
the green grass and the white daisies were waving in
the summer wind, and have looked upon those gray
and russet walls, and upon those lovely arched casements,— among the most graceful ever devised by human art,— round which the sheeted ivy droops, and
through which the winds of heaven sing a perpetual

requiem. I have seen the shadows of evening slowly gather and softly fall, over the gaunt tower, the roofless nave, the giant pillars, and the shattered arcades of Fountains Abbey, in its sequestered and melancholy solitude, where ancient Ripon dreams, in the spacious and verdant valley of the Skell. I have mused upon Netley, and Kirkstall, and Newstead, and Bolton, and Melrose, and Dryburgh. And, at a midnight hour, I have stood in the grim and gloomy chancel of St. Columba's Cathedral, remote in the storm-swept Hebrides, and looked upward to the cold stars, and heard the voices of the birds of night, mingled with the desolate moaning of the sea. With awe, with reverence, with many strange and wild thoughts, I have lingered and pondered in those haunted, holy places; but one remembrance was always present,— the remembrance that it was the Catholic Church that created those forms of beauty, and breathed into them the breath of a divine life, and hallowed them forever; and, thus thinking, I have felt the unspeakable pathos of her long exile from the temples that her passionate devotion prompted and her loving labor reared.

It was natural, therefore, that I should be allured by your invitation,— should be attracted to the votaries of this Catholic Club, to whom such relics are sacred, and to whom such thoughts, however inadequate, may not seem entirely vain. It was especially natural that I should be attracted to this society, assembled to honor an old friend, who, in every walk of life, has borne himself with dignity and ability, and who stands now, without blemish and without reproach, at the white summit of his noble career. Rich in scholarship, copious and delicate in humor, accomplished in jurisprudence, eloquent, faithful, and just, Judge Daly merits every plaudit that respect can prompt or love can utter. I am indeed grateful to be allowed to add my humble homage to your more eloquent and more worthy tribute. In my youth I was a lawyer, a member of the Suffolk bar, in Boston (though never in practice), when Goodrich and Loring, Hallett and Prince, Bartlett and Rufus Choate contended in the forum, and when Nash, and Bigelow, and Metcalf, and Shaw were illustrious upon the bench. Joel Parker, Emory Washburn, and Theophilus Parsons had been my teachers; and, if I learned nothing else in those distant days, I learned to reverence the glorious science of the Law, and to appreciate the attributes of a great jurist.

It is a comfort to think that such homage as you are offering to-night has not been withheld till it could no longer gratify the mind or cheer the heart of the friend whom you delight to honor. Tributes of this kind, amid the tumult of our busy civilization, are not too frequent. The day declines; the darkness draws on; the Old Guard is fast passing away. Its members may well be mindful of each other, while there is yet time. I did not intend a speech, but only to express my sympathy and my gratitude; and I cannot more fully say what I feel than by repeating one of my poems, which, although not originally intended for an occasion, may, perhaps, be considered appropriate here. It is called

## THE SIGNAL LIGHT.[1]

The lonely sailor, when the night
O'er ocean's glimm'ring waste descends,
Sets at the peak his signal light,
And fondly dreams of absent friends.

Starless the sky above him broods,
    Pathless the waves beneath him swell;
Through peril's spectral solitudes
    That beacon flares — and all is well.

So, on the wand'ring sea of years,
    When now the evening closes round,
I show the signal flame that cheers,
    And scan the wide horizon's bound.

The night is dark, the winds are loud,
    The black waves follow, fast and far;
Yet soon may flash, through mist and cloud,
    The radiance of some answ'ring star.

Haply across the shuddering deep,
    One moment seen, a snowy sail
May dart with one impetuous leap,
    And pass with one exultant hail!

And I shall dearly, sweetly know,
    Though storm be fierce and ocean drear,
That somewhere still the roses blow,
    And hearts are true, and friends are near.

Each separate on the eternal main,
    We seek the same celestial shore;
Sometimes we part to meet again,
    Sometimes we part to meet no more.

Ah, comrades, prize the gracious day
   When sunshine bathes the tranquil tide,
And, careless as a child at play,
   Our ships drift onward, side by side !

Too oft, with cold and barren will,
   And stony pride of iron sway,
We bid the voice of love be still,
   And thrust the cup of joy away.

No comfort haunts the yellow leaf!
   Wait not till, broken, old and sere,
The sad heart pines, in hopeless grief,
   For one sweet voice it used to hear.

Thought has its throne and Power its glow,
   And Wealth its time of transient ease;
But best of hours that life can know
   Are rose-crowned hours that fleet like these.

Let laughter leap from every lip!
   To music turn the perfumed air!
Ye golden pennons, glance and dip !
   Ye crimson banners, flash and flare !

On them no more the tempest glooms
   Whose freed and royal spirits know
To frolic where the lilac blooms
   And revel where the roses blow !

But lights of heaven above them kiss,
   As over silver seas they glide —
One heart, one hope, one fate, one bliss —
   To peace and silence, side by side.

# JOSEPH  JEFFERSON

# Joseph Jefferson.

## THE POET AND THE ACTOR.

SPEECH AND POEM AT A DINNER IN HONOR OF
JOSEPH JEFFERSON, GIVEN BY THE COLONIAL
CLUB OF NEW YORK, MARCH 31, 1898.

MR. PRESIDENT AND GENTLEMEN OF THE
COLONIAL CLUB:

I AM indeed grateful for the privilege of participation in this beautiful tribute of affection and honor to a great actor and a noble person, and I heartily thank you for the kind welcome with which the mention of my name has been received. As I gaze upon this impressive spectacle, as I consider the motive that has prompted this assemblage and the spirit with which it is animated — a motive and a spirit suggestive and stimulative of all high thought and noble emotion — I can but regret that no power of eloquence is within my reach, fitly to express the meaning of this scene or the feeling which it inspires. Something, however, I would say of the many precious memories that throng upon my mind, and especially of one memory, that comes upon me with peculiar force at this time, of a great personal, representative experience. I am think-

59

ing of a lovely summer night, more than twenty years ago, in the old town of Stratford-upon-Avon, in the heart of England. The sky was cloudless; the winds were hushed; the river was flowing sweetly, like music heard in a dream; and, as the knell of midnight floated away from the dark and venerable tower, the ancient streets, so quaint and so cleanly, were vacant and silent, under the cold light of the stars; and presently the comrade of my walk, laying his hand gently upon my arm, said to me, in a low and reverent tone, that I shall never forget, " This is the place." We were standing before the house in which Shakespeare was born, and my companion was Joseph Jefferson. Most men, under such circumstances, would have spoken much: my wise and gentle friend said those few simple words, and said no more. For a long time we stood there, in silence, and then, silently, we walked away. The remembrance of that solemn hour is often in my thoughts; for as I look back across the long period of our friendship — a period of well nigh forty years — it seems to me that, not once but many times, he has been present, at supreme moments of my life, still leading me to shrine after shrine of nobility and beauty, and still saying to me, in the same spirit of sympathy, awe, reverence, and worship, " This is the place."

It sometimes happens that one man is divinely ordained to be a guide and a blessing to others. We do not well understand either the source or the nature of his celestial faculty, but we call it poetic genius, and we accept it with gratitude and with delight. Joseph

Jefferson has exercised poetic genius in the art of acting, and in that way he has been a guide and a blessing to thousands of people, all over the English-speaking world. It was not only natural, it was inevitable, that this great actor should dedicate his life to the service of poetry and beauty, for that mission was his inheritance. In the long artistic annals of his race, extending over a period of more than one hundred and fifty years, each succeeding picture is one of ever-growing romance and renown. The baleful echoes of Culloden were still sounding across the Scottish border, when young Thomas Jefferson rode from Ripon to London — there to become an actor in the company of Garrick, and to found the Jefferson family of actors upon the stage. Washington was President of the United States when, crossing the Atlantic, in quest of fame and fortune, the second Jefferson began his career in the American theatre — a career that bore him to the highest eminence, and hallowed his name not only with admiration, but with love. The American stage had felt the impetus, and had begun to rise and broaden under the influence of Cooper, Edwin Forrest, the elder Wallack and the elder Booth, when the third Jefferson obtained and held an honorable place among the actors and managers of his day. An auspicious fate, amid the horrors of the San Domingo rebellion of Toussaint L'Ouverture, spared and saved the lovely girl who was destined to become, in the ripe maturity of her beneficent womanhood, the mother of the fourth Jefferson, and thus to enrich our civilization and to bless our lives with the consummate

comedian whom, this night, we are assembled to
honor.   Thus through succeeding generations that
legacy of genius has been transmitted and that minis-
try of beauty has been prolonged.  The first Jefferson,
dead for ninety years and more, sleeps in the shadow
of the gray cathedral of Ripon.   Not many months
ago it was my fortune to stand beside his grave, on
which the grass was rippling and the sunbeams were
at play; and as I gazed upon that scene of peace I
could but reflect upon the brilliant days of David Garrick and Margaret Woffington, when that sleeper was
in the pride and glory of his youth, with Dodd and
Bannister for his comrades, and Fanny Abington for
his sweetheart, and Edmund Burke and Goldsmith
and Gibbon and Doctor Johnson for his auditors.
But the past is always blended with the present, and
nothing in this world is ever ended here.   At this moment I am carrying a little box of golden shell which
once was owned and carried by the poet Byron, dead
since 1824, and in it there is a piece of the hair of
Sarah Siddons, the idolized actress of her age, dead
since 1831; and you, to-night, hearing the voice of
Joseph Jefferson, have heard a living echo from the
great English days of Queen Anne, when Bolingbroke
led the senate and Marlborough led the field, when
Cibber was bearing the sceptre of comedy, when Congreve was writing his plays and Fielding his novels,
and when poetry commingled thought and fancy,
philosophy and satire, imagery and wit, in the melo-
dious cadences of Prior and in the crystal couplets
and the burning rhetoric of Pope.

In the days of Robert Wilks, and in the later days
of Spranger Barry and David Garrick, there were but
two important theatres in England, and all the good
actors were concentrated in one or the other of those
two houses. In the days of Hodgkinson and Anne
Brunton in America there were but three important
theatres in the whole country. In our day the theatres are numerous, and the good actors are widely
scattered and diffused. There is a public for tainted
trash and tinkling nonsense, but there is also a public
for the noblest poetry and the finest art; and when
we remember the one we shall be wise not to forget
the other. You are all familiar, no doubt, with the
reply of the old woman to the minister who had asked
for her opinion upon the doctrine of total depravity.
" It is an excellent doctrine," she said, " if people would
only live up to it." At the present time there are indi-
cations that the people who support some of the theatres are living up to that doctrine, in the fullest degree.
While, however, we observe the prominence of theatrical trash, we must not ignore the golden record of
dramatic art. Charlotte Cushman and Mrs. Bowers,
Edwin Booth and Lester Wallack, Lawrence Barrett
and John McCullough, Mary Anderson and Ada
Rehan, Henry Irving and Ellen Terry, Charles Coghlan and John Hare, each and all presenting works of
the highest character, have, each and all, obtained the
amplest recognition and the most brilliant success; and
Joseph Jefferson, after a career of more than sixty
years, is the most admired, the most beloved, and the
most popular of all the actors of his time. No fact

could possess more significance nor convey a more
practical encouragement; for this great actor has
never paltered with falsehood, nor sacrificed the right
to the expedient, nor addressed the baser public, nor
taken his law from the multitude; but, from first to
last, he has been true to his mission, as an apostle of
poetry and beauty.    In earlier years, as some among
my hearers are aware, he acted scores of parts, long
since discarded and forgotten, but for a long time he
has wisely restricted himself to characters in which he
is peerless.    Chief among those characters is Rip Van
Winkle; and when I mention that name I call up
before you the blithest, the most romantic, the most
pathetic figure of the modern stage.    All the extremes
of life are comprised in Rip Van Winkle: youth and
age, laughter and tears, happiness and misery, the
natural and the preternatural.    Even the environment
is composed of contrasts, for it passes from the "settled
low content" of the rustic cabin to the desolate mountain peak, solitary beneath the awful loneliness of the
empty sky.    Other actors played the part before Jefferson played it — Flynn and Parsons, Chapman and
Hackett, Yates, Isherwood, and Burke — and other
actors, no doubt, will play it, when he is gone: but no
other actor ever invested it with the charm which is
the magic of Jefferson — the charm of poetry.    In that
one word is the secret of his victory and the reason of
his greatness.    It cannot be analyzed — for poetry is
elusive, and not to be captured by a definition.    We
only know that it arouses the imagination, touches the
heart, and ennobles the mind.    Some persons indeed

there are to whom it speaks in vain. Standing before
one of the pictures of Turner, a censorious artist said
to that great master: " I cannot see such color as that
in nature." " No," said Turner, " you cannot see it;
don't you wish you *could?*" Happy the man who
possesses humor to cheer and beautify his passage
through this mortal life, and poetry, to open upon his
spiritual vision the promise and the glory of the life to
come! I have passed the most of my days in the
study of human nature and in the observance of those
artistic forces which, from all directions, are liberated
to act upon mankind; and I declare, as the result of
all that I have seen and known, that the mission of art
is the revelation and interpretation of beauty, and that
the chief obligation of the artist, whatever be his field,
is to show the ideal to be emulated, and not the horror
to be shunned. Joseph Jefferson has fulfilled that obligation, and in doing that he has lived a beneficent
life and has crowned his honored age with the love of
his fellow-men and with the spotless laurel of an illustrious renown.

Not very long ago I wrote a poem in honor of Jefferson, but I have never spoken it in his presence.
Let me so far encroach upon your kindness as to repeat it now:

12

## JEFFERSON.[1]

The songs that should greet him are songs of the mountain —
 No sigh of the pine-tree that murmurs and grieves,
But the music of streams rushing swift from their fountain,
 And the soft gale of spring through the sun-spangled leaves.

In the depth of the forest it woke from its slumbers —
 His genius, that holds every heart in its thrall !
Beside the bright torrent he learned his first numbers —
 The thrush's sweet cadence, the meadow-lark's call.

O'er his cradle kind Nature — that Mother enchanted
 Of Beauty and Art — cast her mantle of grace ;
In his eyes lit her passion, and deeply implanted
 In his heart her strong love for the whole human race.

Like the rainbow that pierces the clouds where they darken,
 He came, ev'ry sorrow and care to beguile :
He spoke — and the busy throng halted to harken ;
 He smiled — and the world answered back with a smile.

Like the sunburst of April, with mist drifting after,
 When in shy, woodland places the daisy uprears,
He blessed ev'ry bosom with innocent laughter —
 The more precious because it was mingled with tears.

Like the rose by the wayside, so simple and tender,
 His art was — to win us because he was true ;
We thought not of greatness, or wisdom, or splendor —
 We loved him — and loving was all that we knew !

He would heed the glad voice of the summer leaves, shaken
 By the gay wind of morning that sports through the trees —
Ah, how shall we bid that wild music awaken,
 And thrill to his heart, with such accents as these ?

How utter the honor and love that we bear him —
   The High Priest of Nature, the Master confest—
How proudly yet humbly revere, and declare him
   The Prince of his Order, the brightest and best !

Ah, vain are all words !    But as long as life's river
   Through sunshine and shadow rolls down to the sea ;
While the waves dash in music, forever and ever ;
   While clouds drift in glory, and sea-birds are free ;

So long shall the light and the bloom and the gladness
   Of nature's great heart his ordainment proclaim,
And its one tender thought of bereavement and sadness
   Be the sunset of time over Jefferson's fame.

# II

# ACADEMIC SPEECHES

## 1891–1896

"AND WHAT ARE ALL THE PRIZES WON
TO YOUTH'S ENCHANTED VIEW?
AND WHAT IS ALL THE MAN HAS DONE,
TO WHAT THE BOY MAY DO?"

—OLIVER WENDELL HOLMES

# YOUTH AND OPPORTUNITY

# Youth and Opportunity.

SPEECH DELIVERED AT THE THEATRE IN STAPLETON,
STATEN ISLAND, JUNE 19, 1891.

AS I look upon the faces of these young students, I
do not perceive in them any sign of insuperable
reluctance that our oratorical exploits should be cut
short. Nor does that surprise me. Young people
may not always be studious of books, but they are always studious of change. They do not consciously
value the present; they crave the future. Nothing in
the passing moment suffices for the youthful mind,—
which looks ever toward the joy that is promised and
the hour that is to come. I remember my experience
when I was a school-boy, in far-off years, in the old
city of Boston,— how often it happened, on a summer
afternoon, as I sat in the school-room and, gazing
through the open windows, saw the green, waving
branches of the great elms, and the long, fresh grass
rippling in sun and breeze, that my thoughts would
drift away from the teacher, and the task, and the hum
of study, winging their flight across the sparkling crystal of Boston's beautiful harbor, to Fort Independence,
and Governor's Island, and Point Shirley, and the
rest of those engirdling jewels—

> The isles that were the Hesperides
> Of all my youthful dreams.

13                          73

So true is it,— and ever has been, and ever will be,—
as your poet Longfellow has told you, that

A boy's will is the wind's will,
And the thoughts of youth are long, long thoughts.

Long as they are, however, they are not long enough
to reach and grasp the great and golden fact, which can
only be learned by experience, that there is no blessing
in life so precious as the Opportunity of Youth.  Shades
of the prison-house may indeed begin to gather, as the
poet Wordsworth says they do, about the growing boy :
yet now, if ever, he possesses freedom.  Care has not
laid its burden on his spirit.  Doubt has not chilled
his hope.  Worldly strife has not embittered his mind.
Everything that comes to him now comes with a smile.
Never yet has he heard, in the silence of his sorrowing soul, those words which are the saddest in human
speech: " It is too late."  Does any youth ever realize
his privilege ?  Does any youth ever reflect and
comprehend that this is the period when defects of
character may be modified or removed ; when errors
of conduct may be avoided, and sometimes may be
repaired ; when the mind may be fed with knowledge
and the soul exalted with beauty ; when " the world
is all before him, where to choose " ?  The almost uni-
versal testimony of dejection and regret, in mature
years, is the melancholy answer.  " If I could only be
young once more," cries the veteran, " if I could only
live my life over again, how different it would be ! "

Not that the days of childhood and school are the
best days !  That notion is only one of the many

prosperous platitudes that conventional usage has
made respectable. "Where ignorance is bliss, 'tis
folly to be wise." But ignorance is not always bliss.
Knowledge sometimes is bliss — and where knowledge
is bliss 'tis folly to be ignorant. These beginners,
these young adventurers upon the ocean of life, I
doubt not, have many days in store for themselves,
brighter and happier than any that ever yet they have
known — days when, with developed and matured
faculties and the ample equipments of learning, taste,
and experience, they enter into the kingdom of wisdom, which is power; of love, which is life; of active virtue, which is honor, conquest, glory, success!
But the surpassing privilege of youth is the unfettered
spirit, the uncompromised intellect, the boundless opportunity. The page is yet unsullied. The pathway
lies clear and open in the sunshine. The blue heaven
rears its dome of splendor and of promise, without
one cloud to hint of peril or storm. And, even as
now, in these beautiful days of June, the world that
opens to their eager, youthful gaze is a wilderness of
roses that sway and murmur in the summer wind.

What of the future? What will you do with
your lives? We, who are older, who have lived
longer and traveled further, are usually ready enough
with our counsel: but it is your ideal that must
lead you now, and not the advice of others. Honor
and truth we take for granted. "I would be virtuous," said an old philosopher, "though no one
were to know it, just as I would be clean, though no
one were to see me." The book of commonplace pre-

cept need not be opened here. Yet there is one word of counsel which now more than ever,—in a Pagan age of denial and democracy,—ought to be spoken to the youth of America. Be yourselves, and never abandon your noble aspirations! You cannot live in absolute independence of the world. You must have affiliations with other persons: but it is not imperative that those affiliations should be numerous, and you have it within your power to make them select. You are under no obligation to imitate others or to do as others do. You ought never to permit your minds to be inundated with the ignorance, the crudity, and the vapid chatter of commonplace persons. Do not too much reverence the Past. Old burdens that have rolled from the shoulders of weary and dying men and women should not be taken up again by you. It is your life that you must live; it is not theirs; and now that they rest from their labors, let their works follow them. Neither must you suppose yourselves enjoined to assume the burdens that other persons have created, in the present day. Let those attend to grievances who have them, and do not allow your spirits to be dejected, your hopes darkened, and your lives encumbered with the vices, the errors, the follies, and the weakness of failures and of fools. It is, no doubt, pitiable and deplorable that failures and fools should exist and suffer; but they must not be permitted, merely because they exist and suffer, to drag you also into failure and folly. Respect the sanctity of your souls, and beware of superfluous contact with other lives.

For it is only the temporary and the expedient that are gregarious. In every great moment of life, in every time of insight or inspiration or crisis, the human being is alone. The object of education, therefore, should be the development and building of an original, noble, adequate character,— not simply a preparation for industrial pursuits, but an armament for everlasting life. The occupations of this world, however important, are transitory. The soul of man is immortal. Other views, I am aware, are entertained. People who claim to be practical, but are only narrow, are never weary of declaring that education must be sensible and not visionary. An effort to worry the public mind on that subject is a part of the errant activity of the complacent Man of Business, all the world over, and it has been so, at periodic intervals, for many years. I remember its pernicious existence long ago, — the jealous sneer at what was called "book-learning," as opposed to what was called practical knowledge of affairs; meaning thereby cotton, iron, coal, the stock exchange and the revised statutes. Not long since (in 1890), in the newspapers of New York, that epidemic of commonplace burst forth with uncommon virulence, and various individuals, in every case possessed of more wealth than wisdom, apprized us that scholastic training is superfluous, because it aims to furnish an equipment wholly in excess of what is requisite for business. My old friend William Warren, the comedian, used to tell, in his inimitable way, a story about a pompous, conventional tradesman, who was addressing the pupils of a Sunday-school. "I knew a little boy," he said; "who always obeyed his mother, always washed his face in the morning, always came early to Sunday-school, and never stole an apple! And where do you think that good boy is now?" To this inquiry a small voice piped out an answer — "In Heaven, sir." "No, sir," cried the disgusted orator, "not in Heaven! He's *in a store!*" That is the mental drift of those enemies of the higher education. To their minds the chief end of man is to get himself employed in a store. They are what Joseph Jefferson called "the selfish-made men of our time." They recall the remark of an old cynic, Henry Clapp, Jr., who said: "If you want to know what God Almighty thinks of money, look at the men to whom he gives the most of it." Perhaps, however, the sensitive perturbation manifested by those button-makers, those disciples of the grocery and the till, is a good sign. Certainly the fact is significant that the sensitive feeling is all on one side. Educated men are not worried. If education has not always given them wealth, it has given them blessings that no prodigality of wealth can buy; and by this token they know that the province of education is not to train young people for business, but to embark them upon life,— of which business is only an incident. The best wisdom of the wisest of mankind has always taught that lesson. Make your business tributary to your mind, and not your mind subservient to your business. "The world is too much with us," cried Wordsworth. Do not defer to the world, said Matthew Arnold:

> For they, believe me, who await
> No gifts from Chance have conquered Fate.
> They, winning room to see and hear,
> And to men's business not too near,
> Through clouds of individual strife
> Draw homeward to the general life.

Judgment will differ as to the question of education, but there is one subject upon which we can all agree — and that is, our obligation to the young. For some persons within the sound of my voice the roses have already been gathered, the sunshine has begun to fade, the music is dying into silence. Life, for some of us who are gathered here, has taken its settled shape and hue, and it cannot signify much, and it will not signify long, which way the current flows or whither the clouds may drift. But the green leaves follow the sere, and the fragrance of nature and the rapture of life are still in the world. To our tired eyes the scene grows barren and gray; but to the eyes of the children it is bright and beautiful.

> Ah, shield the little hearts from wrong,
> While childhood's laugh is ringing;
> And kiss the lips that sing the song,
> Before they cease their singing.[1]

When the record is made up and we look back upon the past, it is not the memory of what we have done

[1] Lines from a poem by Miss Harriet McEwen Kimball, of Portsmouth, New Hampshire, whose devotional poetry is not less beautiful than sincere, and whose character and life are an honor to human nature and a blessing to all who know them.

for ourselves that will comfort and strengthen us, but the memory of what we have done for others.

The portal through which I entered into the service of the Staten Island Academy was that of calamity and bereavement. The Library that my wife and I have established here commemorates our beloved son Arthur, who perished, in a sudden and lamentable manner, in January, 1886. It is natural that parents should cherish their children as excellent beyond comparison and precious beyond value. I think, however, that I utter the conviction of all who knew him when I declare that, in brilliancy of mind, gentleness of manner, sweetness of temperament, beauty of person, and the exquisite and indescribable charm of genius, Arthur Winter was extraordinary and unique. His life, in this world, lasted not quite fourteen years, and every moment of it was a blessing. For his mother and for me the world is changed and darkened since he went away, and it can never be the same that once it was. I must not, however, speak more than these few words about him now.

> His part in all the pomp that fills
> The circuit of the summer hills
> Is, that his grave is green.

And yet, not altogether so; for he was more than worthy of the monument that we have erected, and time will more and more testify, in the growth and the worth of this institution, as the years drift away, how rich is the legacy of beneficence that the community inherits from genius and goodness that are consecrated

by sorrow and immortalized by love. The noble work
that he might have done in the world, had his life
been spared, can only now be conjectured; but as long
as this memorial endures the influence of his gentle spirit
must still be active for the welfare of others, and
therefore it will outlast the lives of all who mourn
for him, and survive even the regrets of affection and
the tears of grief.

> To live in hearts we leave behind
> Is not to die.

In the making of the Library I have been guided by
one thought. I wished to give to other children what,
if he had lived, I should have given to him. The use
of this collection of books is not limited exclusively to
the academy. The public also, and especially the
actors, may claim kindred here and have their claim
allowed. The books are such as persons with bright
minds can read. A resolute effort has been made to
exclude dullness. In my childhood it was my misfortune to be restricted, for my reading, to the convivial
companionship of such works as the " Night Thoughts "
of Dr. Young, the melancholy numbers of Henry
Kirke White, the versified preachments of the un-
fortunate Cowper,— whose life was darkened and
whose mind was well-nigh ruined by the blight of Cal-
vinism,— and a remarkable compound of elegies by
Gray and Mason, Yalden on Darkness, Dr. Porteus
on Death, and Dr. Blair on The Grave. From the
natural consequence of brooding over these refreshing

14

compositions it was difficult to recover; and later,
when they had been left behind, I had still to endure,
for some time, the weight of "Paradise Lost" and
the somnolent didacticism of "Rasselas, Prince of
Abyssinia." Nobody told me of such authors as Cowley, Herrick, Shelley, Keats, Moore, Burns, Scott, and
Byron, and it was only by chance that I was presently
liberated into the celestial world of Shakespeare. In
directing my efforts, therefore, and in guiding those of the
dear and honored friends among the actors and authors
who have aided me in building up the Arthur Winter
Memorial Library, I have striven to assemble such
creations of literature as will inform, elevate, strengthen,
and cheer; such books as will impart pleasure as well
as wisdom, and happiness as well as virtue; such books
as will be read with delight and remembered with
affection; such books as are a blessing and not a
burden.

I must trespass no further upon your patience. Other
voices are to be heard — voices that I am sure you
will rejoice to hear. One of them, Erastus Wiman,
speaks to you with the authority of a man of affairs,
glad and grateful, however, that he can turn away from
the strife of the practical world, to bear his testimony
here, as he has borne it elsewhere, to the imperative
necessity of educational discipline, the importance of
learning, and the dignity of the scholastic life. The
other, George William Curtis, speaking to you from
the noble eminence of laureled scholarship and beautiful art, weaves yet again the welcome spell of matchless eloquence, turning the memory of other tones to

oblivion, and pointing with new emphasis the lovely thought of Milton:

> How charming is divine philosophy!
> Not harsh and crabbéd, as dull fools suppose,
> But musical as is Apollo's lute,
> And a perpetual feast of nectared sweets,
> Where no crude surfeit reigns.

# THE IDEAL IN EDUCATION

# The Ideal in Education.

SPEECH DELIVERED AT THE THEATRE IN STAPLETON,
STATEN ISLAND, JUNE 17, 1892.

IN these proceedings the part that has been assigned
to me is simple, and I venture to hope that my
performance of it will meet with your approval, if for
no other reason, because it will be brief. As President
of the trustees of the Staten Island Academy I am to
deliver the diplomas of the institution into the hands
of the students who are graduated here to-day ; and,
in behalf of their instructors and of my official associates, I am to wish, for these brave young spirits,—
these adventurous mariners, just embarked upon the
ocean of untried experience,— a prosperous voyage, a
peaceful haven, and a safe deliverance out of all the
perils and tribulations of human life. That wish is
deeply felt and it is soon spoken. " *Nil mortalibus
ardui est.*" Speed onward and be happy! Shakespeare, who says everything for us so much better
than we can say it ourselves, has given us a word for
this hour, among the rest :

> Upon your sword
> Sit laurel victory, and smooth success
> Be strewed before your feet !

With that aspiration I might consider my duty fulfilled. It has, indeed, been suggested that I should

87

proceed further and should address this audience upon such topics as the occasion naturally involves. The friendly makers of that suggestion, however, have but imperfectly considered, or have not considered at all, the formidable obstacle with which I am confronted. George William Curtis, who was to have spoken, is, unfortunately, kept away by illness, and, practically, I am requested to fill the place of the most accomplished orator in America. It is a task that far transcends my powers. I could not hope even to echo the music of that magical voice. The utmost that I could do would be to honor,— as, with all my heart, I do,— the exalted ideal of character, conduct, and scholarship of which he is the conspicuous and consummate image. His presence would have been a kindness and a benefit: his absence is a loss and a sorrow. Yet his absence unseals the lips of homage, and, at least, I may speak of his example. In no better way than when I point to our illustrious fellow-citizen could I denote the ideal of excellence toward which our desires and labors in this institution are directed — the excellence of absolute integrity; of inflexible principle; of profound and incessant devotion to duty; of ample scholarship and a broad mind; of that intrinsic virtue of character which imparts dignity and power to individual life, and that sensibility, refinement, and gentleness which are its surpassing crown of grace. I know that I shall speak the unequivocal sentiment, not of this assemblage only, but of the community, when I exclaim, in the beautiful words of the great Roman poet,

Ibimus, ibimus,
Utcunque praecedes, supremum
Carpere iter, comites parati.

When I had the privilege of speaking to you, last
year, in this place, I urged the superlative importance
of the higher education, I deplored the custom of its
depreciation, peculiar to a class of business men who,
without learning and without culture, have neverthe-
less acquired wealth, and who therefore indulge the
delusion that they are successful in life. My views
upon that subject remain unchanged. Yet I would
not be supposed to underrate the importance of executive ability or of a suitable training for practical
affairs. The natural tendency of mankind is toward
self-indulgence, selfishness, and sloth. It is only by
sleepless vigilance and resolute activity that a virtuous
social progress is stimulated and maintained. Nothing is more important to society than the man of
action who is controlled by wisdom and animated
by a noble purpose. It has long been observed of
the scholar that he is also the hermit. Men of fine
spiritual strain and of high intellectual attainment are,
usually, reclusive. They do not like close contact
with affairs. They are contented to be spectators.
They dwell apart — as Goethe did, and Niebuhr, and
Emerson. They see the errors of the vagrant human
race, and sometimes they indicate them. They consider their duty fulfilled when they have shown the
true principle and the right path, and they do not
wish to be any further troubled. They, generally, do
not expect to see anything made right; — and that is

15

natural; because, for the most part, the world has always passed them by unheeded. They are relegated to solitude and isolation, and they are content. Not until the weakness of age came upon him did that wise philosopher Emerson, for example, show the least impatience because his ideas were not practically adopted and applied. He was satisfied with the diffusion of influence upon the thought of his time. All his days he could look onward, to the great Hereafter, when we shall see wisely and clearly, and be at peace.

It may happen, however, that the scholar is also the man of action, and then indeed there is reason for public gratitude. If truth and beauty are assailed, he will defend them. If right is trampled down, he will raise it up. If ignorant, swarming numbers threaten,— as in Great Britain and in this Republic of ours they do threaten,— to overwhelm and destroy the safeguards of a rational civilization, he will oppose them, he will quell their tumult and enforce their obedience. Honor, therefore, to the practical man! Yet, since scholarship is a weapon not less than a grace, I see not any reason why he who possesses the potentiality of action should not also be regnant in the domain of thought. Let us augment the chances of social welfare by the widest possible diffusion of the equipments and blessings of learning and of art. The higher a man's spiritual and intellectual development,— the ampler his resources of knowledge and of trained ability, the greater his mastery of the experience of the past,— the more trenchant and the more puissant and splendid must be his capacity for helping the progress

of his fellow-men! Practical esteem for practical results is not a new idea. The moderns, with all their
boasting, do little except to rediscover and reaffirm
the ideas of the ancients. Respect for executive force
and labor did not originate with the class that now
assumes to bear its banner. It was, and it ever has
been, the feeling and the purpose of the scholar. I
will mention one denotement of it. More than seven
centuries ago, in the reign of King Stephen, and while
his war with the Empress Maud was still raging, a
synod of the clergy, who were the scholars of that
time, was held in the ancient city of Winchester,— the
king's brother, the astute and formidable Bishop
Henry de Blois, presiding,— and in that august ecclesiastical assembly, representative of all that was best
in the thought and culture of the age, it was formally
decreed that the same privilege of sanctuary that ap-
pertained to the Church should also appertain to the
Plough: and thereupon, solemnly, with lighted torches
in their hands, those monks pronounced the awful sentence of excommunication upon all persons who, from
that day forward, should molest or injure any laborer
in agriculture. Labor has often assailed learning, but
learning has always been the protective friend of labor.

Discrepancies of theory, however, are merely super-
ficial. Nature is above art. Truth survives error.
Things fall into their places without regard to opinion. A conspicuous recent assailant of the higher
education, for instance, is Mr. Andrew Carnegie.
Actions, it is said, speak louder than words: it might
be added that they speak a different language. Mr.

Carnegie has declared that he can dispense with the classics and with all that is implied in the university scheme of classical education. Yet I observe that Mr. Carnegie's highest personal ambition is to be recognized as an author. I observe that the weapon he uses against the higher education is a weapon drawn from its own armory — the weapon of literary style: an implement of thought that he might use with more than his present fluency if he had been trained in those classical studies which he decries, and of which, perhaps, he is not the most competent judge. I remember, also, that the objects of Mr. Carnegie's zealous admiration are those apostles of the intellect, Matthew Arnold and Herbert Spencer,— both of whom he entertained when they were in America. And, finally, I remember that when, with Mr. Carnegie, the practical work had been done,— when the great fortune was accumulated, when the man of business and of wealth wished to insure an actual, permanent, unassailable, indestructible result,— he founded libraries; he built a college ; he started what will one day be a grand picture-gallery ; and he established a superb Academy of Music in the metropolis of his adopted land. That exemplifies the law of mind, the organic, elemental law of spiritual life, operating independently of all crude theories and transient, ephemeral moods :

> For nature, crescent, does not grow alone
> In thews and bulk ; but, as this temple waxes,
> The inward service of the mind and soul
> Grows wide withal.

From the operation of that elemental law there is, ultimately, no escape ; but the predominance of spiritual truth may be facilitated by environment. There are times when a hard, cold, or mean environment becomes intolerable. In youth the right environment is imperative. Nothing so much conduces to the development of character in the right direction. Nothing tends so much toward the economy of force. Nothing so directly contributes to the building of a beautiful life. Youths who are rightly surrounded at the beginning are often saved from errors that it would cost a lifetime to repair.

I have often been called a dreamer. I hope the word is true. The dream that comes to me when I muse upon the future of this institution is part a memory and part a vision. I remember an ancient city, sleeping in the sunshine, on the mountainous banks of the rapid Moselle. I see again, on its embowered crag, the colossal fragments and ivy-mantled walls of the most romantic if not the grandest ruin in Europe. In the far distance glimmers the sparkling Rhine. Around me towers a glorious coliseum of the pine-clad hills. The wind of summer, fragrant with spice and balm, is blowing from the Black Forest, and once again I hear the heavenly music of those golden bells of Heidelberg which are the sweetest in the world. Standing in that venerable place, I stand at the cradle of learning, which also is its monumental shrine. I remember the pensive tranquillity of Stratford-upon-Avon. I see again the gray tower of the ancient Guild Chapel, in which the youths

of King Edward's school annually assemble for their
closing day; and, as the organ sounds and the hymn
of worship floats upward to heaven, I know they will
gaze through the arched casements that Shakespeare
saw, and will look toward the sacred spot, less than a
hundred feet away, where the greatest of all poets
drew his last breath and closed his eyes forever upon
the world. I remember the monastic peace and the
celestial majesty of the close of Canterbury,— the lofty
elms, the brooding rooks, the ivy-mantled masonry of
the middle ages blent with cosy dwellings of a gentler
period and a softer taste, and that stupendous tower
which rises like a pillar of silver into the sunshine of
heaven,— and I see the boys of King Henry's school,
in cloister and chapter-house and sanctuary, surrounded
with the most august and impressive objects and associations of historic renown. And, thus remembering
and beholding what temples of culture and beauty
have been reared for the children and students of other
lands, I dream of a time when, upon yonder hillside,
overlooking your beautiful bay, will rise the gables
and turrets of the stateliest building that ever yet, in
all this region, wisdom and art have devoted to the
sacred service of education —which is the service of
freedom, of religion, of benevolence, of gentleness,
and of steadfast and immutable belief in man's supreme
and superb destiny of everlasting development and
progress, through the countless ages of immortal life.

And now, my young friends,— completing a cere-
mony which has been too long delayed,— I place in
your hands the diplomas of your academy. Your

days have been happy; but many happier days are in store for you than any that ever you have known. Let these memorials be to you the souvenirs of youthful friendships and of precious ties. Let them constantly remind you of the time when your opening lives were dedicated to the service of truth and beauty. To that service be faithful forever. And as often as you look upon these tokens let them admonish you that education is never completed; that as long as you live the opportunity of growth in knowledge, wisdom, and virtue will keep an equal pace with life. I part from you with the beautiful thought of Longfellow:

> Bear a lily in your hand!
> Gates of brass cannot withstand
> One touch of that magic wand.

# THE TRUTH IN EULOGY

16

# The Truth in Eulogy.

SPEECH DELIVERED ON CURTIS MEMORIAL DAY,
AT THE STATEN ISLAND ACADEMY,
FEBRUARY 25, 1895.

THE last word is to be spoken by me, and for that reason I venture to believe it will be welcome. Exacting duties have prevented me from carefully preparing an address for this day, and I shall ask your indulgence if I utter my thoughts precisely as they come into my mind. It is always, however, a dangerous experiment. I remember, in a talk with George William Curtis upon this subject, that he said to me: "I am always glad when it is somebody else who is to speak," and he told me that once, at a banquet, a prominent person said to him: " Do you prepare what you have to say at these dinners." Curtis replied that he did. " Well," said the other, " I do not." And then Curtis added, with that sweet smile of his which many of you so well remember, "When he came to address the meeting I found that he had told the truth." I dare say you will derive much the same impression from the careless speech that I shall utter now.

A great observer of life, the poet Byron, wrote that:

> Men are the sport of circumstances, when
> Those circumstances seem the sport of men.

Circumstances of affliction and sorrow caused me to found, in this institution, a memorial library, led to my election in the board of trustees, and thus, indirectly, made me the chief officer of the corporation. Since ever I have believed anything I have believed that education is the corner-stone of society, but I never expected to be personally associated with the cause of education. From the earliest moment when I became connected with this institution I have labored with all my heart and strength for its advancement. I have especially desired that there should be, in this academy, a home influence, a home atmosphere, an atmosphere of kindness, gentleness, refinement, and beauty. I have desired that teachers should be liberal and noble in their methods of tuition, and mild and reasonable in their methods of discipline, and I have desired that pupils should be docile, obedient, mindful of their opportunities, and studious to improve them — for the privilege and the glory of youth come but once, and not till they are gone do we know how precious they were. That has been, and is, my ideal. We all have ideals, and howsoever they may be marred or defeated by the hard experience of life, I think we shall be wise to hold fast by them, and cherish them.

One reason why I have wished that the life and the character of our honoured and lamented friend Curtis — his beautiful character, his beneficent life — should be urged upon your attention, as often as the anniversary of his birth recurs, is the fact that he possessed, in an eminent degree, those great virtues, especially necessary in studious life, and precious in all

life — forbearance and patience. I have a little dreaded,
however, lest much insistence upon the example of
Curtis might cause our eulogy of him to seem monotonous and tiresome. Nothing is more easy than to
make the name of a good man tedious in the ears of
eager youth. When George Peabody died, in England, many days elapsed before his body was brought
home and his obsequies were completed : whereupon
there was a reference to the subject, in a western news-
paper,— a reference intended to be sympathetic,—
and the editor said : " Such a long time has passed
between the death of Peabody and his burial, and the
newspapers have been so full of the subject, and so
much has been said about him, that we could almost
wish he had not died." There is always the danger
that people in general, and especially young people,—
who live in hope and not in memory,— may grow
weary of hearing Aristides called the Just.

History and biography are prone to extreme views.
If a man is to be denounced as bad, he is made so bad
that we feel he never could have existed,— at least in
the temperature with which we are acquainted. Look,
for instance, upon the character of Richard III. The
genius of Shakespeare has laid upon that character
a blight which it is impossible to remove ; yet nothing
is more certain than that two-thirds of the stories
told about Richard III are untrue. The story, for
example, that he murdered his wife, is ridiculous.
Their marriage was a love-match, and no two people
ever lived more happily together than Richard and
his Anne. The story that he murdered Henry VI, in

the Tower, has been exploded by the clearest evidence. Consider that much-married man, Henry VIII. When I first read about him and his wives I was amazed at the number of his marriages, and at the surprising elasticity of spirit with which, in spite of such deplorable ill-luck, he succeeded in keeping alive the flame of hope in his royal breast. And so, I was quite prepared, when the truth came, as it did at last, when Mr. Froude published the evidence, to learn that those marriages were political, and that it was a political policy that sacrificed King Henry VIII upon the altar of matrimony.

As with the bad men, so with the good. We have all been reared in the belief that if there ever was an angel out of heaven it was William III, who accomplished the revolution of 1688, in England. An angel he may have been, but he was one of the most colossal schemers of whom history preserves the record, and he possessed the additional accomplishment that he could call Heaven to witness his duplicity, and did not hesitate to do so. When his plot against his father-in-law was on the point of completion, his message to his most intimate friend said, simply : " I have not the least intention to make an attempt on the crown, and I pray God, who is powerful over all, to bless this, my sincere intention."

Think of the injustice that has been done to the stately and splendid character of Washington. You will find in the library Mr. Weems' " Life of Washington," and you will find in that book,— there printed for the first time,— the story of the cherry tree and the hatchet, a pure invention, a yarn that its maker took care not to publish until the immediate relatives of Washington had passed away. I do not know any exalted character that has been subjected to more ill-usage. Were it not the character of one of the greatest of men, it would have been seriously impaired in the esteem of posterity, by the "goodies" who have so smirched it with their fatuous insipidity. When I was a youth, I saw a large picture in a shop window in Broadway, representing the Republican Court. In the centre stood the Father of his Country, and beside him stood his mother. One of that lady's hands was laid upon his shoulder, while the other pointed to an eight-day clock, which had recorded the hour of nine. Beneath the picture was an inscription, consisting of words which she was supposed to be saying, in the presence of the Republican courtiers: "Come, George, it is time to retire! Late hours are injurious!" To hang such a fringe of Sunday-school ornament upon the imperial character of Washington is little less than a sacrilege.

Curtis was a reticent man, and some people thought him a cold man. He was not effusive, but it would be a grave injustice to consider him a formalist or a "goody." One of the pioneers who went to the California gold fields in '49, records that one day he had placed a cloth across the window of his hut, so that he might change his apparel and shave, when he was astonished to see the cloth suddenly pulled down and to hear a voice which loudly inquired: "What is going on here so —————— private?" That is a tendency in American life. There must be no individual privacy. He who is not gregarious is supposed to be aping the airs of aristocracy. Curtis not only dwelt apart, but his life was ruled by the sternest moral principle. Whatever might happen, he stood for the right, and he felt, with his friend Lowell, that

> They are slaves who dare not be
> In the right, with two or three.

I should like to linger upon the career of Curtis as a writer and speaker, but I have said much upon that theme elsewhere, and you have heard much upon it from others. Curtis had a high standard of rectitude, and by that standard he regulated his conduct and tested the conduct of others. But he was never a bore, either moral or intellectual. He did not pose as a model. He neither prattled precepts nor distributed tracts. He was fastidious, and, in an eminent degree, self-contained, and, as he lived under the strain of continual intellectual labor, he was, to some extent, isolated; but no man looked with more charity upon the faults and frailties of humanity; no man more deeply sympathized with the joys and sorrows of common life; and no man more earnestly desired, or more faithfully labored to promote, the happiness of his fellow-men. As I think of him, I repeat the words of his friend Longfellow, by whom he was dearly loved:

> O, though oft depressed and lonely,
> All my fears are laid aside,
> If I but remember only, .
> Such as these have lived and died.

# THE IDEAL IN LIFE

# The Ideal in Life.

SPEECH DELIVERED AT THE THEATRE IN STAPLETON, STATEN ISLAND, JUNE 18, 1895.

AS often as this anniversary comes around it brings a sense of relief and peace. The work of the academic year is finished. The long ordeal of anxiety and endeavor is past. The goal has been reached and the toilers may rest. Like pilgrims ascending a mountain-side, who pause, at noonday, in a grateful shade, and, with equal serenity and pleased indifference, gaze downward upon the smiling valley far below, and upward to the cloud-swept summits far above, we feel that a portion of our toilsome journey is happily completed, and that now, for a little while, we can be idle.

> The sun is in the heavens, and the proud day,
> Attended with the pleasures of the world,

and nothing remains but to listen to the ripple of the brook, the rustle of the branches, and the gentle whisper of the summer wind.

It will be well for us, however, not to forget that equally in the hour of repose and in the hour of action the development of individual character must proceed,

107

and that, under all circumstances, the inexorable obligation of duty remains unchanged. Spiritual, moral,
and intellectual advancement is the law of human
life. The mind that does not aspire and advance
will deteriorate and recede. At a moment like this,
therefore, the chief consideration which presents itself
to every thoughtful observer is that of the solemn responsibility, and, at the same time, the splendid privilege of youth. It is an old and hackneyed theme, and
yet for each successive generation it is vital, para-
mount, and absorbing,— and therefore, if its importance be considered, it is forever new. Thousands of
eager spirits have asked the question, in times that
are past, and thousands will ask it in times that are to
come,— What is rightfully expected at our hands, and
what shall we do with our lives?

The youths who are graduated here to-day are so
much nearer than they were to an active participation
in the cares and labors of the world. Other youths
will follow them, year after year, passing through the
same portal of joyous expectation and entering upon
the same dubious and dangerous highway of action,
emulation, and strife. Many trials await those adventurous spirits, but also, as we gladly trust, much
happiness awaits them; and to that fortune they are
committed, with all our blessings and with all our
prayers! No man can foresee the future; and so the
best counsel that experience dictates can only speak
the old heroic watchwords,— Courage, Hope, and
Cheer! It is all crystallized in the golden lines of
Shakespeare:

Look what thy soul holds dear! Imagine it
To lie that way thou go'st, not whence thou com'st:
Suppose the singing-birds musicians,
The grass whereon thou tread'st the Presence, strew'd,
The flowers fair ladies, and thy steps no more
Than a delightful measure, or a dance.

There has not been a time, within my knowledge, when that auspicious admonition was more needed than it is in these hard, glittering, boisterous days, by those who are entering upon the active pursuits of life. The age upon which they are cast is one of painful transition, of agnosticism, of the aggressive, self-assertive encroachment of numbers, and of seething popular tumult. In almost every direction, conflict and noise! In almost every quarter, luxury, profanity, vulgarity, and pretentious mediocrity! The cities are resonant with hideous clangor, and overrun with locomotive agencies of electrical massacre! The country is populous with political quacks and crazy socialists! Leaders of thought, however, have hailed this time as one of splendid achievement,— and this hour is not one for controversy, or even for dissent. The music of your festival should not be marred by a single discordant note. I will only venture to remind you that, after more than seventy years of continuous and amazing scientific development, the dominant influences of the age are more material than spiritual; and, without disparaging science, I should wish to urge that materialism,— promoting selfishness and closing the portal of hope,— is a fruitful cause of evil, and to declare that nothing is so essential to the young

as fidelity to the spiritual principle and inflexible devotion to the ideal. Whatever be the characteristics
of the age, its votaries must confront the hour. I
know not how they could be better armed than with
the sacred purpose to preserve, to the end of their
days, the romance and the beauty of their youth,—
with all its sweet illusions and all its glorious beliefs,
—and to keep themselves unspotted from the world.

There are, indeed, moments when the philosophy
of the ideal seems visionary; when the disheartening
force of the commonplace seems to overwhelm everything with platitude and dullness; when "the seamy
side" of life comes uppermost, with an effect that is
almost comic. I was speaking to an old friend of
mine, in England,— the Duke of Beaufort,—and with
enthusiastic interest, about that famous ruin, Tintern
Abbey. "Make a visit to me at Troy House," the
Duke said: "Come when there is the harvest moon,
for then the place is at its best; and we will go there
together, and see the ghost." And then he added:
"Tintern is a part of my property, and it lately cost
me a thousand pounds to dig the rubbish out of it."
To us that venerable ruin is associated with historic
and romantic traditions and with the sublime poetry of
Wordsworth. To the owner it is, at times, an object
of mere pecuniary solicitude. So goes the world.
There is a commonplace side to everything; but there
is also an ideal side — and it is only by fixing our
eyes upon the ideal that we are able to forget the
toils and cares of a laborious existence and to bear
with patience the ills of mortality.

It is not devotion to a fantasy that I would advocate: it is devotion to the intellect; to learning; to
purity, nobility, simplicity, beauty; to the life of the
spirit, which no worldly mishap can ever defeat! Examples of that devotion might readily be drawn from
the history of literature. Such a book as William
Gifford's Autobiography,— usually prefixed to his
translation of Juvenal,— is worth more to the young
than pages of precept. But I must not linger upon
examples. Amid the vicissitudes of experience, devotion to the ideal is the only sure refuge. At the
outset of life it is natural that the future should be
viewed with anxiety; but this anxiety is often mis-
placed and useless. Every youth must find a vocation, but the building of character is more important
than the choice of employment. When I review the
past, and recall the companions of my youth, and
consider the victors and the vanquished,— who has
been exalted and who has fallen by the way,— I am
almost persuaded that the control of circumstances is
well-nigh impossible. Most persons who have ar-
rived at the autumn of life have rested upon that conclusion. That chord of memory was deftly touched
by Thackeray, in his quaint "Ballad of Bouillabaisse":

> There's Jack has made a wond'rous marriage;
>   There's laughing Tom is laughing yet;
> There's brave Augustus drives his carriage;
>   There's poor old Fred in the Gazette;
> On James's head the grass is growing —
>   Good Lord! the world has wagged apace,
> Since here we set the claret flowing,
>   And drank, and ate the Bouillabaisse.

But, however the world may wag, the fine spirit never falters. Whatever may be the burdens laid upon it, the fine spirit rises to the ordeal, and meets them, and bears them. Whatever the sorrows that darken the world of man, the fine spirit looks through the darkness, and sees beyond it the eternal sunshine of the world of God. Hold fast, therefore, by the spirit that is within you! Cherish your aspirations! Trust in the dreams of your youth! The ships that sailed at morning will all come home before the dark. Life will have trials, and much that time may give will, in time, be taken away; but the hour will never come that can take from you the proud supremacy of your intellect, the rich treasures of your learning, the integrity of your character, the purity of your honor! That is true success!

> Who misses or who wins the prize?
> Go, lose or conquer as you can;
> But if you fall or if you rise,
> Be each, pray God, a gentleman!

Four years ago a voice that we all loved was heard in this place, speaking to cheer our young adventurers upon their morning march. We did not then know that we were hearing the honored Curtis for the last time — that this, for us, was indeed "the setting sun and music at the close." If we could have known it, how sacred every word would have seemed to be! how precious the counsel! how solemn the hour! I know not if it will ever be my privilege to address this academy again. To you, the graduates, let me ex-

press my earnest wish that the lesson of my parting
words may sink deep into your hearts, and always
abide there. You have labored long and well, and
you are graduated here with the approbation of your
teachers and with the sympathy and delighted favor of
your friends. Take from my hands these diplomas
that you have merited so well; and take from my
lips the heartfelt wish that your lives will be successful
and happy! Parting is always sad,— but the sadness of this parting will soon be forgotten. Not so,
I profoundly hope and believe, the purpose with which
you now set forward, to fulfil, by steadfast, unswerv-
ing, passionate fidelity to noble ends, the golden
promise of your beautiful youth. I cannot better
conclude this address than with the wise admonition
of Longfellow, commending the example of the builders
of old :

> Let us do our work as well,—
> Both the unseen and the seen ;
> Make the house where gods may dwell
> Beautiful, entire, and clean !

18

# IN MEMORY OF
# GEORGE WILLIAM CURTIS

# In Memory of George William Curtis.

SPEECH DELIVERED AT THE SEMINARY BUILDING, NEW BRIGHTON, STATEN ISLAND, FEBRUARY 24, 1896.

THE trustees of the Staten Island Academy have authorized the present celebration of the birthday of Curtis, and, speaking as their president and representative, I have now to declare their deep sympathy with the motive, spirit, and purpose of this occasion. "The reason of things," said the old English divine Dr. South, "lies in a little compass, if the mind could, at any time, be so happy as to light upon it." Curtis was one of our friends and benefactors, but it is not for that reason that we select his birthday for especial observance. The academy is grateful to all its friends and benefactors, whether living or passed away, but it does not, and cannot, commemorate them. Curtis was more than a friend and benefactor; he was a great and unusual character, and, dwelling for many years in this community, and coming into more or less intimate contact with many of our lives, he left to us a great and unusual example; and, since our cause is education, which aims ever at harmonious development of character and wise conduct of life, it is

117

appropriate that we should, from time to time, recall the image and dwell upon the memory of one whose nobleness was once a living delight, and whose spotless fame is now a hallowed monitor and guide.

The records of biography, ample and widely diversified, present but few men who, living, as Curtis did, for nearly three score years and ten, developed themselves in a manner so perfectly symmetrical, and exerted upon society an influence at once so strong, so gentle, and so pure. His vocations were journalism, literature, politics, and oratory, and in all of them he was beneficent, because in all of them the exercise of his splendid abilities was inexorably and invariably governed and directed by a clear and fine sense of duty. It would be superfluous here to specify his talents or enumerate his achievements. The word for this hour and this place is simply a reminder of the beauty of his life. He lived for others, and the loveliest attributes of his nature were his sweet and cheerful patience and his exquisite refinement. His mind was invincibly anchored upon what he has himself defined as "that celestial law which subordinates the brute force of numbers to intellectual and moral ascendency," and to the last, and in the face of every adverse occurrence, he believed in the ultimate triumph of virtue and beauty in the ordination of human affairs. The presence of such a man is, at all times, a blessing; the memory of such a man, in the present time of insensate luxury, vacuous vulgarity, and the insolent tyranny of ignorant numbers, is an inexpressible comfort. As

I think of his example, I remember the noble words of Longfellow :

> The star of the unconquered will,
>   He rises in my breast,
> Serene, and resolute, and still,
>   And calm, and self-possessed.

For the abuses of this period, I am wishful to believe, as he believed, will pass away. Our hope is in the cause of education, which he represented, and for which we labor. As that cause advances, the people will learn that they are not wise, virtuous, and noble simply because they happen to be born, but that much self-discipline is essential to make them adequate to the duties of citizenship and worthy of its rights. As that cause advances, the discordant elements of our hybrid population will become subdued and harmonized, and we shall hear no more of "the Irish vote," or " the German vote "; of murders on election day ; of thieves and assassins elected or appointed to public office; of Indians robbed and slaughtered; or of negroes hanged upon trees and tortured with fire. As that cause advances, the press will cease to be,— what, for the most part, it has become,— an odious chronicle of small beer and a hideous, primer-like picture-book for hare-brained fools; while the theatre, which plays so large a part in contemporary social life, will present spectacles that ennoble and cheer, instead of scenes that sadden and disgust. As that cause advances, our highways may be relieved of the baleful engines of racket, destruction, and sudden death with which they

are now furnished, and something like a normal con-
dition of the public ears and nerves may be restored.
As that cause advances, profane and filthy language
will be no longer heard in our streets and our public vehicles, as it is now, and the great American
pastimes of spitting, swearing, and bragging will
happily be discarded. As that cause advances, the
right of voting will be properly restricted and the
intelligence, and not the ignorance and folly, of the
nation will prevail in its government; the cackle of
silly laughter at all serious things will cease to be heard;
and the love and reverence that bind the human heart
to the fireside of home and to the altar of God will
blossom in a civilization of honorable industry, gentle
manners, dignity, and peace.

Swift fly the years and rise th' auspicious morn!

Bayard Taylor, in 1869, said these words:

We have relaxed the rough work of two and a half centuries,
and are beginning to enjoy that rest and leisure out of which the
grace and beauty of civilization grow. The pillars of our
political fabric have been slowly and massively raised, like the
drums of Doric columns, but they still need the crowning capi-
tals and the sculptured entablature. Law and right and physical
development build well, but they are cold, mathematical archi-
tects; only the poet and the artist make beautiful the temple.
Our natural tendency, as a people, is to worship positive material
achievement, in whatever form displayed; even the poet must
be a partisan before the government will recognize his existence.
So much of our intellectual energy has been led into the new
paths which our national growth has opened,— so exacting are
the demands upon working brains,— that taste and refinement of

mind and warm appreciation of the creative spirit of beauty are only beginning to bloom, here and there, among us, like tender exotic flowers. " The light that never was on sea or land " shines all around us, but few are the eyes whose vision it clarifies. Yet the faculty is here, and the earnest need. The delight in art, of which poetry is the highest manifestation, has ceased to be the privilege of a fortunate few, and will soon become, let us hope, the common heritage of the people.

More than a quarter of a century has passed since those words were uttered, and as we look upon our " Doric columns," emblazoned with the great names of the several bosses, together with the various and illustrious Mikes and Barneys by whom our government is infested, our legislation bartered, and our politics disgraced, we are able to reflect that we still possess the blessed privilege of hope.

In the commemorative oration on Curtis that I delivered at the Castleton, on February 24, 1893, I said these words upon literature:

" The mission of the man of letters is to touch the heart; to kindle the imagination; to ennoble the mind. He is the interpreter between the spirit of beauty that is in Nature and the general intelligence and sensibility of mankind. He sets to music the pageantry and the pathos of human life, and he keeps alive in the soul the holy enthusiasm of devotion to the ideal. He honors and perpetuates heroic conduct, and he teaches by many devices of art — by story and poem, and parable, and essay, and drama — purity of life, integrity to man, and faith in God. He is continually reminding you of the goodness and loveliness to which you may attain; continually causing you to

19

see what opportunities of nobility your life affords; continually delighting you with high thoughts and beautiful pictures. He does not preach to you. He does not attempt to regulate your specific actions. He does not assail you with the hysterical scream of the reformer. He does not carp and vex and meddle. He whispers to you, in your silent hours, of love and heroism, and holiness, and immortality, and you are refreshed and strong, and come forth into the world smiling at fortune and bearing blessings in your hands."

Curtis was, first of all and most of all, a man of letters; yet in whatever aspect you please to contemplate his life you find him always the image of integrity, simplicity, and taste. He was a representative American gentleman, and no man of his time more completely embodied the essential virtues of the American character. The heroes of English history whom he had selected as his models, and whose example he kept constantly in view, were Sir Philip Sidney, John Milton, and John Hampden. The American whom he most revered was Washington, and there was in his nature a strong infusion of the reticence, the continence, the coldness, the calm endurance, and iron resolution,— in a word, the inherent, stately aristocracy,— for which Washington was remarkable. He believed in "the rights of man," in the liberty which is not license, in equality before the law; but he did not believe that "the rights of man" are obtained by gregarious wallowing in the mire of vulgarity. He would have equalized society, not by degrading the lofty, but by raising the low. As a patriot he neither bragged nor " hollered." He knew that the Republic is based upon great principles, which the passage of " Resolutions " can neither hinder nor help. He was not provincial, and, had he been living now, he would have been one of the foremost to repudiate and denounce the hysterics with which the peace of our country has of late [1] been endangered, its intelligence humiliated, and its prosperity marred. In politics he esteemed fidelity to principle as more essential than allegiance to party, and his single aim was to do right, without regard to the consequence. As a journalist he respected the sanctity of private life, he did not publish slop and call it "news," he discussed ideas and policies, and he strove to mould and guide the public opinion, not as a follower, but as a leader. As an orator he preserved and illustrated the high and splendid traditions of Burke, Everett, Sumner, and Phillips. His eloquence was dedicated to the service of truth and beauty, to the commemoration of great deeds, and to the glory of splendid names. In literature he had the purity of Addison and the gentleness of Goldsmith, together with a moral fervor, a cheerful sweetness, and a pensive grace that were his own.

The American authors in association with whose names I treasure that of Curtis are the elder Dana, Washington Irving, Fitz-Greene Halleck and Donald G. Mitchell; not because he resembled them, in all their attributes, but because, like them, he diffused refinement and cheer from a region of meditative

[1] The allusion is to the Venezuela folly.

seclusion. Washington Irving I never saw, but the elder Dana I saw and heard, in my youth, and I remember a glimpse of Halleck. The most interesting of American authors now alive is Mitchell, and he is so because, among other reasons, while profoundly devoted to his art, he is not feverishly solicitous as to the admiration of the world.

The commemoration of such men as Curtis is among the good auguries of our turbulent time, for it means that probity, personal distinction, learning, art, and the graces of life are not wholly unrecognized or unvalued. Thirty years ago not a single monument had been erected in the United States to an American poet. The first monument of that kind ever set up in this country was the obelisk commemorative of Halleck, at Guilford, Connecticut, where he was born and where his ashes rest.[1] Curtis was not distinctively a poet, although he possessed elements of the poetic temperament, but he was a representative man of letters, and his beautiful pages have enriched our literature and our lives. The Staten Island Academy purposes to erect his monument. It will be the Curtis Lyceum, and within it will be placed his portrait and his bust, together with the relics of him that we are able to assemble; and within it, as the years drift away, by speech, by song, by festival, by every form of artistic effort and by every manifestation of innocent joy, all that is finest in the mind and brightest in the beauty of our island will unite to honor him, as he

[1] The Halleck Monument, at Guilford, Connecticut, was dedicated on July 8, 1869.

would have wished to be honored, by association with their happiness, and thus to keep his memory forever green.

Let me close this address with the gentle aspiration of the poet Whittier:

> Our lips of praise must soon be dumb,
>    Our grateful eyes be dim ;
> O, brothers of the days to come,
>    Take tender charge of him !

———

NOTE.—In the course of this address the speaker told humorous anecdotes, and he counselled the students to read only those authors whose writings awaken in their minds a spontaneous, alluring sympathy, and not to expend their time in merely conventional reading. He also repeated, as appropriate to Curtis, the touching lines on Joseph Rodman Drake, written many years ago by Halleck, beginning:

> " Green be the turf above thee,
>    Friend of my better days !
> None knew thee but to love thee,
>    None named thee but to praise."

# THE STATEN ISLAND ACADEMY

1 A WORD OF WELCOME

2 THE INTELLECTUAL PRINCIPLE

3 A WORD OF FAREWELL

# A Word of Welcome.

SPEECH AT THE OPENING OF THE NEW BUILDING
OF THE STATEN ISLAND ACADEMY, AT ST.
GEORGE, NEW BRIGHTON, S. I., JUNE
15, 1896.

A PLEASANT duty,—one of the most pleasant duties that have ever engaged my attention,— devolves upon me now. To you, the teachers and pupils of the Staten Island Academy, now for the first time formally assembled in its new building, I wish to speak a welcome, warm as kindness can make it, to this beautiful and permanent home. You will not expect me to say many words. The occasion, indeed, is one that scarcely calls for speech, because "things seen are mightier than things heard," and because to-day the evidence of our work is seen.

This massive fabric, with its pleasing outlines, its graceful gables, and its romantic aspect, rising, under verdant trees, upon the golden shore of your beautiful Island, tells its own glad story of a noble purpose splendidly fulfilled. This eager assemblage, also, is eloquent of the consummation of a high endeavor. The long and weary years of anxious toil and waiting are ended. The courage that nothing could daunt and the patience that nothing could tire are rewarded now. I welcome you to light and beauty and pleasure; to a habitation of comfort; to spacious halls

and studios, wherein art and luxury will deftly minister to the needs of use; to a library that will make
you intimate with the best of all society, the immortal
minds of every language and of every land.  In one
word, I welcome you to an ideal scholar's home.

The reader of that precious biography, Boswell's
Life of Johnson, is usually amused by the philosopher's description of the vendible brewery of his friend
Thrale.  "It is not," said Dr. Johnson, "merely a
collection of vats and boilers, it is the potentiality of
growing rich beyond the dreams of avarice."  In a
somewhat kindred vein, let me declare of this academy — it is not merely a collection of chalk and
blackboards, of slates and pencils, of the hard and
barren paraphernalia of tuition; it is a temple of culture: and by culture I mean the possibility of a happiness that no vicissitude can alienate, the possibility
of a success that no adversity can mar.  In this
scholastic haven you will, we hope, be happy,— find-
ing the pathways of knowledge pleasant, and laying,
firm and broad and deep, the foundations of an
honorable, useful, lovely life.  Opportunity is an
angel that never comes but once.  That angel has ar-
rived for you; and her face is radiant with promise
and her hands are filled with blessings.  Whether
that promise will be fulfilled, and whether those blessings will be enjoyed, it is, in a great measure, for you
to determine.  Your future will depend upon your use
of the present.

Every human creature, I am aware, acts according
to the trend of character — for that is fate; but even

fate can be modified by the action of the will; and you, who are upon the threshold of life, have now the golden opportunity, if you so resolve, to profit by the lovely environment that others have provided for you, and also by the monition of their experience. That monition would be, to make no error at the beginning. No human being ever entirely recovers from the consequences of a mistake at the start. Heed the warning of those who have preceded you. The highway of human life, which to you seems strange and new, is a beaten track to them. Strengthen yourselves for your long journey, by the acquisition of knowledge, by cultivating the habit of independent thought, and by a devout allegiance to high standards of character, duty, and conduct. Aim always at the highest. It is recorded of the great Admiral, Lord Nelson, that when he was first made a captain, he used to encourage the midshipmen on his quarter-deck, by saying to them, "I am going a race to the mast-head; I hope to have the pleasure of meeting you there." We are all making for the mast-head. May it be your privilege to nail your purple banners of victory to the peak, where they shall float and flash, in the golden glory of the sun, through all the tranquil hours of your long and happy day!

# The Intellectual Principle.

SPEECH DELIVERED AT THE STATEN ISLAND
ACADEMY, JUNE 16, 1896.

JUNE has come back, and with it the abundant
grass, the glistening foliage, and the roses triumph-
ant in the sun.   It is the season of bloom and beauty,
and all nature is exultant and superb.   It is the season
of rejoicing, and rightly and naturally it brings to us
our festival of scholarship and our annual time of rest.
Once more we cast aside our burdens.   Once more
we look to the ocean and to the stars.

> The clouds sail and the waters flow
> Whichever way they care to go,
> And all the sounds of action seem
> Like distant music in a dream.

Shades of regret mingle, indeed, with all occasions
like this, for the reason that these festivals of parting
indicate the flight of time and the incessant and inexorable operations of change.   For some of us — perhaps for all of us — after to-day, nothing will be as
once it was.   In this assemblage, however, the feeling of the hour is chiefly one of gladness.   The dedi-
cation of this noble building marks an auspicious
triumph for the cause of education, and thus for the
welfare of the community, and in that we may well be
glad.

133

When I speak of education, I do not mean merely
the impartment of knowledge, but the development of
the character and the building of the mind. The influence that leads to that result is always a public benefit. Civilization succeeds when it produces commu-
nities that are governed by justice, dignified by intelligence, and adorned by refinement. In parts of the
republic it has amply and brilliantly succeeded; in
others it has failed; and it has failed for want of true
education — the education that exalts the soul above
material things, and that cultivates, not the senses, but
the intellect.

I must not linger upon the shadows of the national
picture, but neither must I disguise from myself that
some of the signs of these times are ominous and sad.
The church seems divided against herself. The political situation is fraught with danger. The populace
of labor views with discontent the spectacle of wealth
concentrated in the hands of a few persons, and would
gladly disperse it. The newspapers, with here and
there an exception, by their reckless appeal to the low
tastes and passions of the multitude, have widely corrupted the public morals and much debased the standard of public intelligence. Developments are everywhere in progress,— notably in the application of
electricity to common life,— which, unless more wisely
regulated, must inevitably, and within a few years,
make us a nation of nervous invalids.

While, however, I believe that ignorance and folly
were never more widely diffused than they are now,
and that levity and coarseness were never more ram-

pant, I also believe that devotion to splendid ideals was never more profound with those who feel it, or more determined to conquer and to rule. The hope of civilization is in the school; and, therefore, the brilliant success of such an enterprise as we celebrate to-day is auspicious, not only for its advocates and promoters, but for society. This is one of many steps in the right direction.

When I have wandered in the old world; when I have roamed among the scholastic cities of England; when I have paused among the groves and avenues of Oxford and Cambridge, and seen those stately temples and palaces rising, glorious, upon those incomparable lawns; when I have mused in the gray and haunted gloom of venerable Winchester; when I have stood awe-stricken beside the ancient towers of the cathedral of Canterbury, while the ivy was trembling on its walls, and the rooks were flying over it, and the western sun was flooding its great windows, and the organ was throbbing in its bosom, like a voice out of heaven, then, deep in my heart, I have felt the passionate desire that this celestial beauty, or something like it, might be communicated to my own land, and made perpetual for the benefit of my people.

That is the spirit in which I have felt, and thought, and written, and labored. That is why I am an advocate and a worker for education; and if it were essential for me to exhort you on this subject (which it is not, because you will be addressed by an honored friend of mine,[1] a far abler and more eloquent voice),

[1] John Foord, Esq.

I should strive to impress upon your minds and memories the enormous importance to a community of having within its centre an institution fraught with the celestial associations of beauty and devoted to the sacred service of learning and art.

In my speech delivered here yesterday I addressed myself to the pupils, with words of friendly counsel. To you, sir, the principal of the Staten Island Academy,[1] I now address myself, with words of cordial congratulation. In every enterprise that I have known there has always been one moving spirit, whose indomitable purpose and incessant industry at last accomplished the desired result. In this academy enterprise you have been the moving spirit. Yours was the steadfast purpose to obtain the new building, and to that purpose the last ten years of your life have been devoted. Your design was worthy of a scholar and a public-spirited citizen, and the fulfilment of it was worthy of an enlightened community. You have labored with exemplary fidelity, and you have conspicuously manifested the virtues of resolution and patience. You now rejoice in ample and auspicious success. That success it is my privilege to crown. With the sanction of the trustees, and in the presence of your pupils and your admiring friends, I now commit to you the custody of this building, and I place in your hands its keys, which are the symbols of your charge. No responsibility in life is more momentous than that which attends the guidance of youth. The influence of the teacher, af-

---

[1] Frederick E. Partington, Esq.

fecting the character and conduct of the pupil, is perpetual. I believe that you appreciate and deeply feel the solemn importance of your vocation, and I have only now to express the earnest hope that your enthusiasm and your zeal will continually be encouraged and cheered by the public sympathy and support, and that, as the field of your labor broadens, your strength will endure and your success increase. May all blessings rest upon you, in the performance of your duty, and upon the institution over which you have presided so long, so ably, and so well.

# A Word of Farewell.

CLOSING SPEECH AT THE STATEN ISLAND ACADEMY,
JUNE 16, 1896.[1]

THE parting moment has come, and I must say
farewell. It is a word that has long been familiar
to my lips; it is a word with which, as the years pass,
we all become sadly acquainted. Life is full of partings
and farewells. It is useless to repine at them: and if
now, in the evening twilight of experience, I were
asked to name the best of all the virtues, I should de-

---

[1] Before saying the farewell word the speaker read the following extract
from an address by Lord Acton, delivered before the University of Cambridge,
England:

"I shall never again enjoy the privilege of speaking my thoughts to such an
audience as this, and on so valued an occasion a lecturer may well be tempted
to bethink himself whether he knows of any neglected truth, any cardinal
proposition, that might serve as his epigraph, as a last signal, perhaps even as
a target. I am not thinking of those shining precepts which are the regis-
tered property of every school; that is to say: learn as much by writing as by
reading; do not be content with the best books, seek side-lights from the
others; have no favorites; keep men and things apart; beware of the prestige
of great names; trust only authorities that you have tested; be more severe to
ideas than to actions; do not overlook the strength of the bad cause or the
weakness of the good; never be surprised by the crumbling of an idol or the
disclosure of a skeleton; judge talent by high-water mark, and character by
low; expect demoralization more from power than from cupidity; problems
are often more instructive than periods. . . . Most of this, I suppose, is un-
disputed. But the weight of authority is against me when I implore you never
to debase the moral currency or lower the standards of rectitude; to suffer no
man and no cause to escape the undying penalty which history has the mission
to inflict on wrong, but to try others by the final maxim that governs our
lives."

139

clare that they are a calm acceptance of fate and a
cheerful endurance of fortune, whatever comes.

New duties await you. New scenes will open before you. Try to make others happy. Try to diffuse
happiness at every step. True success is in the moment. Remember that you are as much in eternity
now as you will be ever, and therefore let your plans
of excellence and achievement be made for to-day and
not for to-morrow. Nothing in human life is so sad as
the blind propensity of almost all kinds of people
to resolve to be something different and better, by and
by. Your hour is now, or it is never.

I request you to take from my hands the diplomas of
the academy. They are not only the certificates of
your scholarship, but of the delight of your parents,
the sympathy of your friends, and the approval of your
teachers. Take them, and with every blessing. You
will be remembered here; and we, in turn, hope that
we may not be forgotten. Fare you well! and, in the
language of the old Bible: "The Lord watch between
thee and me, when we are absent one from another."

# RECORD OF NAMES

## BIOGRAPHICAL RECORD OF NAMES
## MENTIONED IN THE FOREGOING SPEECHES.

Aristides ................................... —— – B.C. 468
Juvenal ....................................Abt. 60 – 140 A.D.
St. Columba ................................. 521 – 597
Empress Maud ....... ...............Abt. 1102 – 1167
Stephen, King of England.................... 1105 – 1154
Henry De Blois............................. —— – 1171
Henry VI., King of England............... .... 1421 – 1471
Richard III., King of England ......... ....... 1452 – 1485
Anne, Queen of England, wife of Richard III..... 1456 – 1484
Henry VIII., King of England................. 1491 – 1547
Edward VI., King of England................. 1537 – 1553
Sir Philip Sidney......... ............. 1554 – 1586
William Shakespeare ......... .... ......... 1564 – 1616
Robert Herrick............................. 1591 – 1674
Richard Burbage .... ......... ......... .... —— – 1629
John Hampden ............................. 1594 – 1643
John Milton ............................... 1608 – 1674
James Graham,                    ⎫
   First Marquis of Montrose  ⎬ ........... .... 1612 – 1650
Abraham Cowley............................ 1618 – 1667
Robert South, D. D ........................ 1633 – 1716
Thomas Betterton........................... 1635 – 1710
John Graham, of Claverhouse, ⎫
   Viscount Dundee            ⎬ .............. 1650 – 1689
John Churchill,                     ⎫
   First Duke of Marlborough ⎬ .............. 1650 – 1722
William III., King of England..... ........... 1650 – 1702
Anne, Queen of England..................... 1664 – 1714
Matthew Prior............................. 1664 – 1721

Robert Wilks ................................ 1666 – 1732
William Congreve. ......................... 1670 – 1729
Colley Cibber................................ 1671 – 1757
Thomas Yalden ............................ 1671 – 1736
Henry St. John,
   First Viscount Bolingbroke } .............. 1678 – 1751
Edward Young ............................ 1684 – 1765
Joseph Miller .. .......... ......... 1684 – 1738
Alexander Pope............................ 1688 – 1744
Robert Blair............................... 1699 – 1747
Henry Fielding ............................ 1707 – 1754
Samuel Johnson ........................ 1709 – 1784
David Hume .............................. 1711 – 1776
David Garrick ............................ 1716 – 1779
Thomas Gray.............................. 1716 – 1771
Margaret Woffington .................... 1719 – 1760
Spranger Barry............................ 1719 – 1777
Adam Smith............................... 1723 – 1790
Sir Joshua Reynolds ..................... 1723 – 1792
Oliver Goldsmith.......................... 1728 – 1774
Thomas Jefferson, Rip's great-grandfather ....... 1728 – 1807
Edmund Burke ............................ 1729 – 1797
Frances Abington ......................... 1731 – 1815
Beilby Porteus............................. 1731 – 1808
William Cowper............................ 1731 – 1800
George Washington ....................... 1732 – 1799
James Dodd................................ —— – 1796
Patrick Henry............................. 1736 – 1799
Edward Gibbon............................ 1737 – 1794
James Boswell............................. 1740 – 1795
Francis Dominic Toussaint L'Ouverture......... 1743 – 1803
Charles Dibdin ............................ 1745 – 1814
Johann Wolfgang Von Goethe.............. 1749 – 1832
Robert Ferguson.......................... 1750 – 1774
Thomas Wignell ........................... 1753?– 1803
Dugald Stewart ........................... 1753 – 1828
George Crabbe ............................ 1754 – 1832

Sarah Siddons ............................... 1755 – 1831
John Philip Kemble .......................... 1757 – 1823
William Gifford ............................. 1757 – 1829
Horatio Nelson, Viscount and Admiral ......... 1758 – 1805
Mason L. Weems ............................. 1759 – 1825
Robert Burns ............................... 1759 – 1796
John Bannister ............................. 1760 – 1835
William Dunlap ............................. 1766 – 1839
John Hodgkinson (Meadowcraft) .............. 1767 – 1805
William Chapman ............................ 1769 – 1839
Anne Brunton (Mrs. Merry, Mrs. Wignell, Mrs.
   Warren) ................................. 1770 – 1805
William Wordsworth ......................... 1770 – 1850
Sir Walter Scott ........................... 1771 – 1832
Samuel Taylor Coleridge ..................... 1772 – 1834
Robert William Elliston ..................... 1774 – 1831
Joseph Jefferson, Rip's grandfather .......... 1774 – 1832
Charles Lamb ............................... 1775 – 1834
Joseph Mallord William Turner ............... 1775 – 1851
Charles Kemble ............................. 1775 – 1854
Walter Savage Landor ....................... 1775 – 1864
Charles James Mathews, the elder ............ 1776 – 1835
Thomas (Abthorpe) Cooper .................... 1776 – 1849
George Barthold Niebuhr ..................... 1776 – 1831
Charles Mayne Young ........................ 1777 – 1856
Thomas Moore ............................... 1779 – 1852
Lemuel Shaw ................................ 1781 – 1861
Washington Irving .......................... 1783 – 1859
Theron Metcalf ............................. 1784 – 1875
Henry J. Finn .............................. 1785 – 1840
Thomas De Quincey .......................... 1785 – 1859
Henry Kirke White .......................... 1785 – 1806
Edmund Kean ................................ 1787 – 1833
John Louis Uhland .......................... 1787 – 1862
Richard Henry Dana ......................... 1787 – 1879
George Gordon Byron (Lord Byron) ........... 1788 – 1824
Fitz-Greene Halleck ........................ 1790 – 1867

James Buchanan .............................. 1791 – 1868
Percy Bysshe Shelley......... ........... 1792 – 1822
William Charles Macready .................... 1793 – 1873
Samuel G. Goodrich........................... 1793 – 1860
James William Wallack, the elder.............. 1794 – 1864
Charles G. Loring .......................... 1794 – 1867
Edward Everett...... . ............. ..... 1794 – 1865
Joel Parker.................................. 1795 – 1875
George Peabody.......................... ..... 1795 – 1869
Joseph Rodman Drake...... .................. 1795 – 1820
John Keats.................................. 1796 – 1821
Junius Brutus Booth, the elder................. 1796 – 1852
Frederick Henry Yates ....................... 1797 – 1842
Theophilus Parsons .......................... 1797 – 1882
Benjamin F. Hallett.......................... 1797 – 1862
Thomas Hood ....... ................... 1798 – 1845
Thomas Barry................................. 1798 – 1876
Henry Placide................................ 1799 – 1870
Rufus Choate................................ 1799 – 1859
Sidney Bartlett ..... ................... 1799 – 1889
James Henry Hackett...................... 1800 – 1871
J. Hardy Prince ............................. 1801 – 1861
William Evans Burton........................ 1802 – 1860
Charles James Mathews, the younger.... . .... 1803 – 1879
Charles B. Parsons  ....................... 1803 – 1871
Ralph Waldo Emerson ...................... 1803 – 1882
Joseph Jefferson, Rip's father ................. 1804 – 1842
Thomas Flynn............................... 1804 – 1849
William Rufus Blake ......... ........... 1805 – 1863
Edwin Forrest........................... .... 1806 – 1872
James Oakes ...................... ........ 1807 – 1878
Henry Wadsworth Longfellow................. 1807 – 1882
John G. Whittier ....................... 1807 – 1892
John R. Scott.... .................. .... 1808 – 1865
John Brougham...... ........... 1808 – 1880
Alfred Tennyson .................. . .... 1809 – 1892
Oliver Wendell Holmes .... .......... ....:.... 1809 – 1894

| | | |
|---|---|---|
| Henry Giles | 1809 – | 1882 |
| John Gibbs Gilbert | 1810 – | 1889 |
| George Tyler Bigelow | 1810 – | 1878 |
| Hezekiah Linthicum Bateman | —— – | 1875 |
| Frances Anne Kemble | 1811 – | 1893 |
| Horace Greeley | 1811 – | 1873 |
| William Makepeace Thackeray | 1811 – | 1863 |
| James Edward Murdoch | 1811 – | 1893 |
| Wendell Phillips | 1811 – | 1884 |
| Charles Sumner | 1811 – | 1874 |
| William Warren | 1812 – | 1888 |
| Charles Dickens, the elder | 1812 – | 1870 |
| Epes Sargent | 1812 – | 1880 |
| John C. Fremont | 1813 – | 1890 |
| Francis A. Durivage | 1814 – | 1881 |
| Henry Clapp, Jr. | 1814?– | 1875 |
| Andrew Jackson Neafie | 1815 – | 1892 |
| Wyzeman Marshall | 1815 – | 1896 |
| Charlotte Cushman | 1815 – | 1876 |
| Charles Fisher | 1816 – | 1891 |
| Edwin L. Davenport | 1816 – | 1877 |
| Joseph Proctor | 1816 – | 1897 |
| James Anthony Froude | 1818 – | 1894 |
| James William Wallack, the younger | 1818 – | 1873 |
| Catherine Farren (Mary Anne Russell) | 1818 – | 1894 |
| John Johnstone Wallack (Lester Wallack) | 1819 – | 1888 |
| Charles Kingsley | 1819 – | 1875 |
| Hudson Kirby | 1819 – | 1848 |
| Edwin Percy Whipple | 1819 – | 1886 |
| James Russell Lowell | 1819 – | 1891 |
| Rachel (Elizabeth Rachel Félix) | 1820 – | 1858 |
| George Eliot (Marian Evans) | 1820 – | 1881 |
| Herbert Spencer | 1820 – | —— |
| Edward Eddy | 1821 – | 1875 |
| Charles T. Congdon | 1821 – | 1891 |
| Charles St. Thomas Burke | 1822 – | 1854 |
| Stephen Gordon Nash | 1822 – | 1894 |

| | | |
|---|---|---|
| Matthew Arnold | 1822 – | 1888 |
| Donald G. Mitchell | 1822 – | —— |
| John Edmund Owens | 1823 – | 1886 |
| Edward F. Keach | 1824 – | 1863 |
| Charles Fechter | 1824 – | 1879 |
| William Wilkie Collins | 1824 – | 1889 |
| Henry Charles Fitzroy Somerset, Duke of Beaufort. | 1824 – | —— |
| George William Curtis | 1824 – | 1892 |
| Richard Henry Stoddard | 1825 – | —— |
| Bayard Taylor | 1825 – | 1878 |
| Adelaide Ristori | 1826 – | —— |
| William Warland Clapp | 1826 – | 1891 |
| Charles Bullard Fairbanks | 1827 – | 1859 |
| Curtis Guild | 1827 – | —— |
| Ulysses S. Grant | 1828 – | 1885 |
| Joseph Jefferson (Rip Van Winkle) | 1829 – | —— |
| Fanny Janauschek | 1830 – | —— |
| Julia Dean | 1830 – | 1868 |
| Elizabeth Crocker (Mrs. D. P. Bowers) | 1830 – | 1895 |
| A. Wallace Thaxter, Jr | 1832 – | 1864 |
| Tommaso Salvini | 1833 – | —— |
| Edmund Clarence Stedman | 1833 – | —— |
| Edwin Thomas Booth | 1833 – | 1893 |
| John Emerich Edward Dalberg-Acton, Baron Acton. | 1834 – | —— |
| Edwin Adams | 1834 – | 1877 |
| Erastus Wiman | 1834 – | —— |
| Harriet McEwen Kimball | 1834 – | —— |
| Marie Seebach | 1834 – | 1897 |
| Samuel Langhorne Clemens (Mark Twain) | 1835 – | —— |
| William Winter | 1836 – | —— |
| Lawrence Barrett | 1836 – | 1891 |
| John McCullough | 1837 – | 1885 |
| Andrew Carnegie | 1837 – | —— |
| Henry Irving | 1838 – | —— |
| Augustin Daly | 1838 – | —— |
| John Hare (Fairs) | 1838 – | —— |
| Francis Bret Harte | 1839 – | —— |

Thomas Hardy .............................. 1840 – ——
Joseph F. Daly........................ 1840 – ——
William Black ....... ................ 1841 – ——
Charles F. Coghlan ...................... 1842 – ——
Edward Dowden...................... ........ 1843 – ——
Helena Modjeska (Helena Benda) .......... ... 1844 – ——
John Foord ...................... ............ 1844 – ——
Adelaide Neilson........................ 1846?– 1880
Ellen Terry ...... ..... .................... 1848 – ——
Sarah Bernhardt .......................... 1850 – ——
Ian Maclaren (Rev. John Watson, D. D.) . ..... 1850 – ——
Frederick E. Partington ..................... 1854 – ——
Mary Anderson (Mrs. De Navarro) .... ...... 1859 – ——
S. R. Crockett............................. 1859 – ——
Ada Rehan ................................ 1860 – ——
James M. Barrie........................ 1860 – ——
Rudyard Kipling .......................... 1865 – ——
William Isherwood ........................ —— – 1841
Arthur Winter............................ 1872 – 1886

The author would express his grateful appreciation of the kind assistance given to him, in his search for authentic dates, by Col. T. Allston Brown, Mr. Douglas Taylor, Mr. Willis Fletcher Johnson, Mr. Francis M. Stanwood, Mr. B. F. Stevens, Mr. Augustin Daly, and Mr. F. E. Partington.— There is scarcely a name in the foregoing Record that has not been, or might not be, the theme of thoughtful essay or pleasing reminiscence.